A STONE IN MY HAND
Cathryn Clinton

CANDLEWICK PRESS

First paperback edition in this format 2010

Translated nursery rhyme from *Gaza: Legacy of Occupation:
A Photographer's Journey.* Copyright © 1995 by Dick Doughty
and Mohammed El Aydi, published by Kumarian Press.
Reprinted by permission of Dick Doughty.

While every effort has been made to obtain permission to
reprint copyright material, we have been unable to trace the
copyright holder of the poem on page 66. The publisher will
be happy to correct the omission in future printings.

The Library of Congress has cataloged the hardcover edition as follows:

Clinton, Cathryn.
A stone in my hand / Cathryn Clinton. — 1st ed.
p. cm.
Summary: Eleven-year-old Malaak and her family are touched by the
violence in Gaza between Jews and Palestinians when first her father
disappears and then her older brother is drawn to a radical group.
ISBN 978-0-7636-1388-4 (hardcover)
[1. Muslims — Fiction. 2. Family life — Gaza Strip — Gaza — Fiction.
3. Jewish-Arab relations — Fiction. 4. Gaza — Fiction.
5. Gaza Strip — Fiction.] I. Title.
PZ7.C622815 St 2002
[Fic] — dc21 2001058423

ISBN 978-0-7636-2561-0 (paperback)
ISBN 978-0-7636-4772-8 (reformatted paperback)

16 17 18 19 20 21 RRC 10 9 8 7 6 5 4 3

Printed in Crawfordsville, IN, U.S.A.

This book was typeset in Granjon.

Candlewick Press
99 Dover Street
Somerville, Massachusetts 02144

visit us at www.candlewick.com

This book is dedicated to three overcomers
who have taught me about life beyond survival:
Dan, Jena, and Marshall.

With special thanks to Norma Fox Mazer,
who nurtured not only the writing,
but the writer, and to Amy Ehrlich and
Erin Postl for their belief in the story.

A Note from the Author

I began writing A Stone in My Hand *in 1998, and in January 2000 I signed a contract for the book. It is historical fiction — the story of a single girl and a single family — and it takes place in Gaza City in 1988 and 1989, when Gaza was under Israeli military occupation. These years were part of the first intifada.*

The intifada, which literally means "a shaking off," was an unplanned uprising of street demonstrations and strikes by the Palestinian people. The first intifada began in 1987 and ended in 1993. A Stone in My Hand *reflects that period of time and is not meant to be a comment on political situations in the Middle East today.*

I am the child of Palestine

I have my cause and I have my rights

When I see my older brother

Taken up into outlaws' hands

I cry out the international cry

That if they shoot me to my death

I'll clutch a stone in my right hand

And never forget the martyrs' cause.

—translated nursery rhyme,
as sung by a five-year-old girl
from Khan Yunis, Gaza Strip

THE ROOF

∞

I am Malaak Abed Atieh, and this bird is Abdo. Abdo lives here on the roof. I sneak him seeds when no one is watching. My sister lives in the smell of the stove with my mother, like the other girls I know, but I do not. I live in Abdo's eyes. I see things my sister and brother will never see. I fly high, high above Gaza City. I soar out of the Gaza Strip. Nothing stops me, not the concrete and razor wire, not the guns, not the soldiers. I stare at them with my hard black Abdo eyes, and they do not shoot me. I am hidden. I laugh at them, but they don't hear it in the sound of the bird. My wings are strong. I dip and dive, stretching these wings, but then I come back to the roof and fold them under me. Someday I may fly away for good, but for now I watch and wait.

My brother, Hamid, is cocky. He always argues with my sister, me, my mother, everyone. I think that when he was born, his mouth was wide open yelling and his hands were in little fists. Yesterday he and Tariq, his best friend, left to play soccer. I followed Hamid. He is easy to follow because his wiry hair sticks out all over and he walks with a strut, like Abdo. They were only halfway down the street when an Israeli soldier appeared at the corner. They ducked into an alley, then came back out with stones in their hands. They shouted at the soldier and ran toward him. They lifted their arms to throw the stones.

I gasped. They could be arrested for that, beaten even. But the soldier lifted his gun over his head, holding it with two hands, and yelled. Hamid yipped and turned and ran into Tariq. Tariq fell over, twisting his ankle under him. Hamid kept right on running. The soldier started laughing.

I helped Tariq limp home. He stared, unblinking, with his stone eyes. He winced with pain, but he didn't speak to me. I didn't speak to him. We are alike in this: we both speak very little.

Hamid brags about being one of the *shabab*; he thinks this makes him a youth fighter in the intifada, which was started by the people of Gaza a little over a year ago.

Last night, he said to my sister, "The young men of Gaza are tired of standing by the road, hoping for a day's job. Waiting, waiting for some Israeli to come up and check our muscles and stare into our eyes. We are not animals. We are *shabab*."

Hamid shakes his fist as he speaks. I just stare at him. He must have heard those words from someone else.

"We are fighters. The stones speak. The soldiers will have to listen." The brave Hamid who left his friend alone in the street. For now, Hamid's biggest fist is in his mouth.

My sister, Hend, looks like my mother. Deep dark eyes, thick straight hair, straight nose, and straight teeth. She is pretty.

I'm not. My nose is too big, like someone punched it in. Probably Hamid did. One front tooth overlaps the other. I don't have straight anything. And my wavy hair flies around my face.

Hend thinks of marriage, and little-beard boy-men. A few months ago when we were on the way to the market, she said, "I will have a wedding bigger than any you have seen."

I laughed. "When, Hend?"

"When the intifada is over; you wait and see," she said. Since the intifada started, there haven't been wedding celebrations in Gaza. How can we have wedding celebrations, my mother says, when there have been so many funerals?

Hamid says, "Will you be rich, Hend?"

"When this trouble is over, this uprising, we'll have the money. You wait and see," she replies. Hend, the wait-and-see girl.

Hamid laughs and laughs. Hend's breath escapes in a hiss. "Why do I even bother to tell you anything? What do either of you know? You are just foolish children."

Who is foolish? I am a girl, but I do not hope for men. I do not wait for weddings. I am not content with cooking and sighs. I go to the roof. I live in Abdo's eyes. I see things my sister and brother will never see. I live in the sky.

"Malaak, come down." I pretend that I do not hear my mother's voice. "Malaak, I know you are there." She will come up on the roof if I am quiet. Her *thump, thump* climbs to me.

She sits beside me, arm around my shoulder. Her eyes become full. Full of salty water like the sea. The Dead Sea. I do not look into them. Instead I kiss the salt on her cheeks. We are sitting in the same place where we sat a month ago when we watched my father walk away.

That day, he was going to look for mechanic work in Israel because he had just lost his job. The garage owner said there were not many cars in Gaza to fix anymore because so many wealthy families had emigrated to other places since the intifada. But my mother works too, and they're saving money to buy a taxi.

Right before the corner, Father turned around and gave me the signal. He shot his fist into the air with his thumb pointed up. This sign means "I am winning." Then he yelled, "See you there in the evening."

I laughed. This meant that even a job in Israel wouldn't change our game. Ever since I was little, I would wait on the roof for my father to come home from work. When I saw him at the corner, I'd make the I-am-winning sign. Then I'd run down the roof stairs on the back outside wall of the house, and in through the kitchen door. Father would race through the street. Whoever got to the front door first was the winner. Usually I won.

That day, my mother and I stared until we saw him no longer. We have not seen him since.

"How is Abdo?" she says. Others would be rid of him by now. But my mother knows Abdo is special. She doesn't touch him.

I hold out my hand, palm up. I place a seed in it. Abdo flies into my palm and pecks it without touching my skin. We look into each other's eyes. Then he flies to my shoulder and sits there.

"He is strong," my mother says. We go downstairs to eat together. She is very quiet. She doesn't speak the rest of the evening. She kisses me on the forehead.

"Sleep, my child." My mother presses my forearm with her hand. I lie down on my mattress and turn toward the wall. Sleep comes quickly.

ABDO

∾

A rooster wakes me. Or is it the voice of the *muezzin,* calling from the mosque, for morning prayer? They crow at the same time. They fight over who gets to wake the people. Today, the rooster won, so I get up before Hend does. She gets up for morning prayer.

When I climb to the roof to feed Abdo, I hear the *muezzin* chanting. It is Friday, the day many men go to the mosque for a sermon and prayers.

"*Allahu akbar.* God is most great! *La ilaha illa Allah.* There is no god but God. *Al-salat Khayr min al-naum.* Prayer is better than sleep."

I'm not so sure that prayer is better than sleep, but only Abdo hears this thought. As I stroke

Abdo, I remember when I first saw him. It was the day after my father left.

On the day that my father left, I went back up to the roof in the evening to watch for him. I had to be there to play the game. I don't remember falling asleep, only that the heavy gravel in my eyes kept closing them. When I woke up the next morning, I was in my room. I was furious. Who had moved me? I went back up to the roof to look for Father. I waited, but he did not come.

Hend kept calling me to come downstairs that day, but I ignored her. I could not leave the roof. I was waiting for Father. He would be looking for my signal.

The last rays of sunset were glinting off the antenna when I heard my mother's footsteps. Her eyes were red. She held her shaking hands in front of her as if she were beckoning me. Her hands were pale, except for the dark purple veins.

"Malaak, I'm so sorry." She stopped, drew in a long breath, and then blew it out through her lips.

"Malaak, your father is missing. He should have been home by now."

What? My father was missing? I thought of the man down the street.

This man had left for work years before, when I was five, and had never come home. People used to say, "Have hope," when they visited his wife. That was the first year. Then people did not speak when they came out of her house. The man had become nothing. Not alive and not dead, nothing. People didn't visit his wife anymore. Would that happen to my father, my mother?

"Only God knows where he is."

No! my mind screamed. Missing men — fathers, brothers — could be dead.

Like my uncle. He didn't come home from work in Jerusalem one day, and finally, a week later, my father's cousin called from Jerusalem to say that he thought he had seen my uncle on TV, on the news. They were covering a demonstration, and the camera had zoomed in on the people in back of the demonstration. A man ran across the street and put his hand on a car door. Then he dropped to the ground. The cousin thought the man was my uncle. It was. He'd been shot. That was why he never came home.

There was a movement behind my mother.

It was a bird.

"Maybe he is in prison," my mother said. "I've heard that the border police were pulling men in for questioning at the Israeli border yesterday. Maybe the police pulled him off the bus. They do not need to have a reason. Maybe."

The bird sat on the corner of the roof, looking at me. I saw that my mother's mouth was still moving. I could see some words, *Maybe hurt . . . hospital . . . dead . . . God forbid.*

But I couldn't hear them. The last word I heard was *prison*. My mind had seized it, and it stayed. I was in a tight, dark place, and the air was being squeezed right out of me. I could not let my mind take in any other words. I

saw the bird, opening and

doing it. I knew the bird

My mother's hands dro

rumpled skirt over and ov

I opened my mouth but my words were gone. Perhaps the bird knew where they were. I walked around my mother and stared at the bird. It stared back. My mother touched my shoulder, but I kept staring at the bird. My mother pressed my forearm with her hand, and then she turned and went downstairs. "May you reach morning in goodness."

That night, I fell asleep on the roof. The bird was watching me.

In the morning, I was awake before anyone else. I went downstairs to get some seeds. I made a row of seeds from my corner of the roof to the corner where the bird was. When I finished, I heard *Abdo* in my mind. I looked up at the bird. It had said its name. That was the message. Just for me.

I waited up there all day. Before sunset Abdo was a few seeds closer, but my father wasn't home. The moon came up, and I stared at it until I heard the *thump, thump* of my mother's footsteps. I pretended to be asleep. She covered me with a blanket and said, "Sleep, my child." She me there. After she left, I sat up.

Abdo pecked a few seeds closer. *Come, Abdo,* I whispered in my mind. *I am patient. I have nothing to do but wait.*

Abdo flew into my hand, ruffling his white feathers and scratching around in my palm. It hurt but I didn't mind. Together we watched for my father to come. I wondered if the bird could find my words, but if Abdo knew where they were, he didn't let on.

We stared out at the houses and buildings that are so tight together, you can hardly see between them. TV antennae crisscross electric wires. Trees are scattered between the old stone-and-concrete walls.

For two weeks, I mostly stayed up on the roof with Abdo. I didn't have school. The Israeli Civil Administration had closed it.

Then my mother said I had to go down in the house with them. "We will wait together," she said in a low, sad voice.

So now I go up to Abdo whenever I can.

THE PIECES

∽

I hear and understand people, but nothing else makes much sense.

Like my feelings. Yesterday when I drank a glass of water, a piece of sadness appeared. During lunch I listened to Hamid tell a story, and a piece of silly laughter settled next to a stab of pain in my ribs. Then in the afternoon, a piece of sunlight made me angry, so I touched my cheek and that made me hum. Such a clutter.

After that first day when I lost my words, I didn't try to speak much. If I did, only bits and pieces of words, sometimes just letters or sounds, came out.

Now I feel, see, hear the words in my mind,

but it is like the front page of a newspaper that someone has torn into little bits. No one can read me. There are too many ragged pieces that don't go together.

My best time is night because I dream in pictures, whole luscious pictures. One night I had a special dream. It was about my father. He went to the moon by jumping from star to star. When he was almost there, he turned and gave me the signal. I signaled back, and then I ran the other way, circling the moon until I caught him and hugged him.

It's been five weeks since I've talked much. Anyway, that is what Hend said earlier today. I don't really know, only that it seems forever. I talk more now, but I don't have much to say.

I feel a scratching on my hand, and I look down to see Abdo. I'm not on the moon in my memories anymore. I am on the roof, and I hear the rumble of the Israeli fighter planes as they go over us. I don't know why they are flying. For practice? For patrol? I grab Abdo and hold him in the crook of my arm. We sit on the blanket by the antenna until long after it is quiet. I shake my fist at the plane's smoke trail.

They will not get me, my mind says to Abdo. *No, I have important things to do. I will visit my father today.* I look into Abdo's eyes.

Soaring above Gaza City,

blue skies everywhere, everywhere.

Skies with no fences, no camps.

I see the prison.

I land on the roof and then find

my father's tiny window. So tiny.

How can anyone live with so little sky?

I take him a piece of the blue.

Now he can live one more day.

I will be back tomorrow,

I tell him.

BARRICADES

It is evening. From the roof I see the last coral streaks fading from the sky. The call for prayer was about fifteen minutes ago. Abdo finishes the seeds on my hand. He stretches one wing, pecks under it, and then he flies to the edge of the roof. He turns his head around to look at me, and I hear sounds of yelling from the street below.

Then I hear Hamid yelling, "Malaak, Malaak!" His feet pound as he runs to the roof. When I see his face, I know that his quick breaths are from excitement, not from fear or hurry. "The men from our street, even the very old ones, are setting up a barricade. I'm joining them, but don't tell Mother or Hend. And if anything should happen to me, give my soccer ball to Tariq. And my note-book of poems is yours, but you are the only one who is allowed to read them. I know I can trust you." He squeezes my shoulders and then runs down the roof stairs before I can do anything. Our house is very close to the next one, but if you are skinny like Hamid and me, you can run between the houses to get from the back alley to the street.

Does he think he will be hurt today? Is that why he is telling me to do these things? Since the beginning of the intifada, people have been set-ting up barricades in the roads to keep out the Israeli soldiers in their armored personnel carri-ers. Someone must have heard that the soldiers are coming our way. My belly jumps. It hurts. I don't want Hamid to be hurt. If Father were here, he would go out there. He would keep Hamid safe.

"Come back!" I yell down at him, but he is running to the end of the street. He probably can't hear me because the men are yelling at each other and dragging things into the street. An old broken refrigerator, a chair with one leg missing.

Hamid stands and watches as the men try to pull over the old sewer pipes that have been there for years. Then he joins the men and pushes the pipes. Soon there is a large barricade at the corner of our street.

"Hamid, Hamid, where are you?" Hend calls from below. Soon I hear Mother. "Hamid, Hamid!" They must have been in the sitting room when he ran downstairs. I hear the pounding of their feet on the roof stairs. Hend runs onto the roof, followed by Mother. They both look toward the refrigerator barricade. My hands are in front of my eyes, but I'm peeking through my fingers. It is getting dark, but I can just see a boy pushing a tire into the road. Another boy stuffs newspaper into it and sets it on fire. When the fire blazes, I see that they are Tariq and Hamid. Mother sees Hamid too.

"There he is. We must get him back inside. There could be gunfire!" She and Hend run down the stairs. The darkness has a shape. It has arms and it is squeezing me. I can't move.

Soldiers appear near the refrigerator barricade,

and I hear shouting. An old man yells, "You will not come on our street with your jeeps and personnel carriers. Go away! We do not want you here!"

"Oh, help, Abdo," I whisper. "There is so much I do not understand. I'm frightened." I can't take my eyes off the street.

"You are a good listener, Abdo, but the only word you ever spoke to me was your name. I wish you would say more." Abdo opens and closes his beak, but no sound comes out.

The soldiers pull down their gas masks. This means they have tear gas. One raises his gun with the tear gas canister on it. I hear the dull thud and pop as the canister flies from the gun. I watch it arc through the sky, breaking a window in a house. White fog mists out the window. I hear a baby screaming. I look away from the window toward Mother and Hend. Mother is grabbing Hamid. Hend is yelling at Tariq.

Oh, Father, come home. Oh, Father, don't you see Hamid?

I turn and look into Abdo's eyes.

᏶

Rising through the smoke,

I streak upward.

I circle the palms with their

open leaves pressed to the sky.

They are calling me to

come sit on them, but I do not.

I ride the shifts in the wind,

higher, then lower, then higher still.

At last I'm free of the fire,

the smoke, the sound of battle.

Free to be with Father.

THE MARKET

∽

"Malaak, come down from the roof now. What are you doing up there anyway? There is nothing up there but birds. Come. It is time to go to the market."

It is the morning after the barricade, and I hurry down to Hend. Hamid joins us. He says he must go with us to protect us, but he is only twelve, a year older than I am, and not much bigger.

Smoke from the tire fires sits on me as soon as I walk out our door. The barricade is still in place, but I'm sure that soldiers will come and make people move it soon.

"The Israelis have put a curfew in place. There was a lot of demonstrating and barricading last night. Not just here. I heard about it this morning on the radio," Hamid says.

He shows us how to squeeze under the refrigerator that is tipped over onto a sewer pipe. As we round the corner, I look up to see that the dome of the mosque is still white. It rises high above the smoke. By the time I get to the school, I feel seasoned by the smoke, like a piece of lamb on a spit. It lingers in my clothes, my skin.

The market street bulges with people. It cracks at the seams like a bag full of flour I carried home a while ago. I see a crooked man sitting at the corner. He is new there. The crooked man has a goat.

My father had a goat too. I remember what he told me: "Ah, Malaak, when I was a boy, we lived in the country in a little village. Jews, Christians, and we Muslims. We lived in the same place, without fighting. Can you believe that, Malaak?" His eyes went far away from me. I put my hands around his face and turned it toward me. I looked into that faraway place.

"Tell me what happened," I said. I'd heard this story before, many times in fact, but I knew he wanted me to ask him.

"My father, blessed be his memory, was the *mukhtar,* head of our village. He had much land and even a car. When he heard that the LEHI, a Jewish unit, had attacked Deir Yassin and massacred many Arabs — men, women, and children — he told the people of our village to flee. Most came to Gaza. My father didn't know that when the war was over, the Israelis wouldn't let us return to our homes. Now our village is gone. The Israelis bulldozed it and built a settlement for Jews in its place."

He shook his head as if trying to rid it of bad thoughts. "Even though the war was over in 1949, my father thought about his decision as *mukhtar* and wondered if he'd done the right thing. He was sad all his life."

"Father, tell me about the goat."

"Ah, the goat. I was only five when we left. I had to leave my pet goat named Orange Blossom.

Of course, he did not smell like a blossom, but I thought if I named him this, maybe he would live up to his name. Would you like a pet goat, Malaak?" I nodded and leaned my head on my father's chest. "Someday we will live in the country, and I will get you a goat."

Now I look into the eyes of the crooked man at the market. He is not so different from me. I pinch his spotted goat, and it bleats. We laugh together, the crooked man and I.

Hend goes on ahead of me. She is haggling with a woman. Buying cucumbers. She moves on to buy flour.

Hamid crosses the street to talk to Tariq and shouts, "Bird Girl, Bird Girl, are you Goat Girl now?" He is laughing, teasing, but I shake my fist at him anyway. Tariq is limping, and his shoulders are hunched. This makes his skinny body look smaller. The wounded dog goes back to his master. Poor Tariq.

Hend turns around and sees me with the crooked man. "Here, carry the flour, Malaak. Stop playing with animals. You are eleven, too old for that." She walks beyond the taxi station. She thinks that because she is sixteen and in secondary school, she is grown-up.

But lately the Israeli authorities have closed the secondary schools a lot. Hend has been working more than she has been in school anyway. She and Mother clean houses for some wealthy people in Rimal.

GUNS

∽

I follow Hend, wrinkling my nose as a new smell hits me. Ugh! Donkey and sweat. An old woman with a sun-soaked face is pulling on a donkey, but it won't move. I run around it, but it kicks out with its back legs. I lose my balance and fall into someone. I hear a grunt, and then I hear, "What are you doing?"

From the ground, I see the black boots and green pants of a soldier. I look up until I see the M-16 rifle dangling against his thigh. My eyes freeze on the gun.

"Here," the soldier says, but before he can say more, I jump up and start running. The soldier is shouting as I turn a corner and hide in an alley. My breath jags. It rips me. My hand is grazed, bleeding. I lean against a wall and slide down. The wall scratches my back. I remember the sight of M-16s pointed at someone else. I close my eyes, but that picture is inside me forever. I cover my ears, but I still remember the sound.

It was when I was walking home from the market with my father, just a week before he left. We turned a corner and saw some young men with their heads and faces wrapped in red-and-white checked *keffiyehs*. These young men are the real fighters of the intifada.

My father pulled my hand. "Come, Malaak. Walk fast." But I looked over my shoulder to see the men write. Their hands cut back and forth across the white wall. A giant red fist grew under their hands, and then the words FREE PALESTINE. Writing pro-Palestinian words is illegal.

A jeep roared. Some *shabah* yelled a warning.

"We can't make it to the end of the street, Malaak," my father said. "Drop down." My father stepped in front of me. I peeked around his legs and saw Israeli soldiers jump out of a jeep, their M-16s pointed at the men.

"Stop!" the soldiers yelled.

My father's legs pressed me back against the wall. It scratched my back. "Close your eyes." My father's voice was hard. I closed my eyes, but I heard the crack of a gun. The jeep started, and my father lifted me up. He carried me like a tiny baby. I was deep in his arms. Rocking in his steps. Safe. "I'm sure it was rubber bullets," he said. He repeated it over and over.

Then Hend's voice breaks into my mind, bringing me back to this alley. Father is not here to pick me up and carry me home.

"Malaak, what are you doing? I've been looking for you." She kneels, dropping her cucumbers. "The soldier was looking for you. He was afraid you were hurt. He meant you no harm." She gasps as she sees my hand. "Does it sting?" She brushes bits of rock off my hand. "Please stop rocking, Malaak. Talk to me, please talk to me. I don't know what to do when you do this."

She smoothes my hair. She pulls me into her arms and she rocks too. Her sighs drift around me. After a time, Hend and I pick up the cucumbers and we go home.

I go to the roof. I open my palm to Abdo. There are no seeds, but he comes anyway. After a long while, I hear my mother calling to me.

"Malaak, I forgot all about the clothes," my mother says. "Quick, go outside and take them down."

I run down the roof stairs to the alley. It is narrow, all mud brown and dull concrete, except for little flags of color. They fly on the line along the back of our house. I take down each flag— a purple shirt, a white scarf, Hamid's blue shirt, and Mother's gray skirt. I fold them carefully. Abdo flies down and sits on my shoulder.

Flying, flying until

I see the lines of clothes.

Rows of shirts, men's shirts, hanging.

Their reaching arms are

long, tangling.

They try to tie me to earth,

but I rip them with my beak.

I fly far, far above

the pieces.

SCHOOL

∽

Hend's movements wake me. She gets up at the sound of the *muezzin*. She goes to the kitchen to do her ritual washing before prayer. I can barely hear Mother and Hend's words, or maybe it is just because I know what they are saying:

"God, Glorified, praiseworthy and blessed is Thy Name and exalted Thy Majesty and there is no deity worthy of worship except Thee. . . ." Their voices fade away.

We live in my grandparents' house. My parents lived with them from the time my parents married. Our house is small and not so wide. That is why I can hear so much, and that is why I spend a lot of time on the roof. Hend and I used to share a bedroom. But now my mother cries at night.

Hend goes to her when she cries. A lot of the time Hend just sleeps with my mother.

Hend's voice comes upstairs, much louder now. "How can you send her to school? For six weeks now she has said so little. She just follows us around like a little lamb following a shepherd."

"I know, but maybe school will help her. Maybe it will give her something besides your father to think about. I spoke to the teacher yesterday and told her about Malaak. She understood. We must try it."

Then Mother yells to me, "Come, Malaak. You overslept. Now you must hurry. It's time for school. The Israeli authorities have opened the schools again, and we don't know how long they will stay open."

I have not been to school since my father left. The authorities closed all the schools the day after that and kept them closed for a long time.

"Malaak, you must be able to read well," my mother says. "You will go to the university, like my sister." Mother is proud of her sister. She is a nurse. She and her husband moved to Egypt, where he got a good, paying job, and now we do not see them anymore.

Hend looks up to our aunt because she met her husband at the university and they married "for love," as Hend says in that sticky voice she uses when she talks of marriage. Families, not love, arrange many matches, but my mother's family is not so traditional.

My mother brings me my school uniform. I pull on the blue-and-white striped dress. Its white collar is spotless.

Hamid walks beside me as we head for school. We both look at a poster of the PLO's Yasir Arafat. It is illegal to put up his posters.

Then Hamid points out a layer of whitewash on the pockmarked old wall of a house a few doors down. "Yesterday it read, LONG LIVE THE INTIFADA," he said. The Israeli soldiers often pull someone off the street and make them paint over graffiti. Even if the person didn't write it.

As we walk, I notice that there are many shades of whitewash. How many ways can I say *whitewash*? Chalkwash on concrete block, creamwash on old white stone, milkwash on cracking masonry.

It is warm in Gaza. Air shimmers up from the road, and the old white stone in the buildings seems to make everything brighter, warmer. Sun, no clouds, no rain.

I remember when the rain bounced off our roof, and I did not want it. I begged Father to stop it. I covered my ears and said, "Father, I want to go outside and play. Stop it. Turn it off."

"Ah, Malaak, don't you know that in Gaza when it rains, it means that God is smiling? He knows how much we need the rain. Come." He grabbed my hand and pulled me outside. "Look up in the sky and feel God's smile." He turned his face to the sky and let the raindrops hit his face. I did too. We opened our mouths and ate the rain.

But now I'm in a back alley. The sewers are horrid today. Hamid runs beside me as I hold my nose and try to make it to the end of the alley on one breath. Then we are back on a main street. I am afraid to go on the main streets because of the soldiers. They've always been around, but mostly they stayed near their barracks. I didn't notice them much. But since the intifada, there are many more units here, and they shoot their guns and beat people.

Sewers or soldiers. Ay! Hamid leaves me at my school and runs on to his.

At school, I take the seat that the teacher points to. It is like starting over at the beginning of the year because we've been gone so long. I sit next to a very big, older girl named Suhara. I look down at my desk and pull out a piece of paper. It is so clean I must write on it. I write my name over and over. I try a curlicue at the beginning and a swirl at the end. My name must look beautiful. Malaak means angel. My father called me his angel.

I'm good at drawing, and Hamid is good at writing poetry. But he doesn't write anymore. He says he is too busy with other things now. He used to show his poems to me, and sometimes I would draw pictures of his poems. I remember the first line of one of them: *Little bird, little bird, why don't you fly?*

And I draw birds on my paper. I cover my paper with birds. All of a sudden, I hear laughter. When I look up, I realize everyone is staring at me. The teacher is walking toward me. My face stings. I'm sure it is red.

"Malaak, Malaak, where are you? I've been calling on you. Why didn't you come up to my desk?"

Suhara is staring at my paper. She says, "She can't hear you because she is in the sky with the birds." She grabs my paper and holds it up. Everyone laughs.

"Enough, Suhara." The teacher takes the paper from Suhara's hand and puts it on my desk. I stare at Suhara. I hate her.

School is finally over. And there is Hamid across the street. He is holding a rope tied around the neck of a little brown-and-white goat. "Here. I thought you might want your own little goat." I laugh and pet the goat. "Actually, I only borrowed him from that man up there," Hamid says. He points to a man ahead of us. He is wearing a brown *jalabiya* and guiding a herd of goats along the street. The man stops at the corner and waits for us to bring the goat to him.

"Thanks," Hamid says. The man has coarse hair, and his long brown robe looks old. It has a large hole near the bottom. There are deep lines in his face, which get even deeper as he smiles at us.

"Sure you don't want to be a goat herder?" he asks.

"I'm sure," Hamid says, "but you could ask her." He points to me and laughs.

"Thank you," I say.

When I get home, I run straight to the roof three steps at a time. I hold Abdo against my school uniform. Abdo rubs his beak back and forth against my collarbone. I picture Suhara next to my desk in the room at school, with her puffy cheeks and heavily shadowed eyes.

"Yes, I am up here with you," I whisper to Abdo, "and that stupid Suhara sits at a desk and stares at other people's papers because there is nothing in her brain to put on her paper."

The sun dazzles off a white dome in the mosque and blinks through the top of the minaret. Even the trees are flecked with light. Gaza is all golden for a moment. I wonder if it is just the tiniest bit like Paradise, where God lives. "I see things Suhara can't see. I will go to places she will never go," I tell Abdo.

ISLAMIC JIHAD

❧

The next day, Hamid and I walk along the street on the way home from school. He stops and talks to a vendor. The man has a full dark beard that can't hide his big yellow teeth. He is selling tomatoes, lemons, and cigarettes. On the next street, Hamid stops to watch two old men playing cards under a stone archway. He speaks to them. And so it goes, all the way home. Everyone knows him. He lives out here, just going from thing to thing. But I've lived mostly from the inside, looking out. I go in the house but Hamid takes off. Hend is watching an Egyptian soap opera. Mother comes home from work at her usual time, before our evening meal.

"I wonder where your brother is," Mother says as we eat supper.

"He's probably out rushing around doing his important *shabab* work," Hend says. By the way she says it, I know that she is making fun of Hamid.

"I'm afraid," my mother says. "There is more tension now. I feel it even in my sleep, and sometimes I wake up with headaches."

My neck is stiff. I rub at the bones in it. Is this tension? Tension seems like a good name for the thing that came into my room and woke me up last night, turning my head from side to side. I could feel its hands on my neck.

The door is flung open and Hamid rushes into the room. His breath comes in short bursts that shake the dust in his hair, his face, and his clothes. We all stop eating and stare at him. "I have been with Nasser. He's been telling me stories. Stories of Islamic Jihad. About how six members of Islamic Jihad escaped from Gaza Central Prison, the slaughterhouse."

I look at my mother. She does not like to hear talk about any of the extremist groups like Islamic Jihad.

"Yes, yes. That happened more than a year and a half ago," Hend says, "and we all know that you look up to Nasser the Brave and hang on his every word. But I'm glad that all he does is tell stories."

Hamid ignores her and goes on. "I suppose you think the PLO is better, but it is just a bunch of groups who don't agree on very much. Arafat just came out on top of the heap. The PLO break down so easily when they are captured. Did you know that Siftawi, of Islamic Jihad, never broke under interrogation?"

Mother takes a bite of cucumber. She chews it slowly, so slowly that I wonder if she remembers it is there. "I like Nasser, and I know he is your friend. I've known his mother for years now, but this is the talk of foolish boys who think these are the stories of bravery. Bravery is not seen in one act. It is measured by the choices and deeds that fill every day of our lives."

She is speaking of my father. I know it. And I

know I will never forget the words. "Bravery is not seen in one act. It is measured by the choices and deeds that fill every day of our lives." I see Father's hand upraised. The thumbs-up sign. My right hand is in my lap. It clenches, forming the sign. I hold it up above the table toward Hamid. *Remember Father,* my hand is saying, but Hamid does not see it.

Remember Father. I close my eyes and we are at the sea. I watch the sand and water trickle through his large rough hands as he scoops up the sea and gives it to me. When I turn and try to give it to Hamid, it is gone. My hands are too small to hold the sea. I open my eyes wide, trying not to blink. But my eyes are oceans, and each blink is a wave that sends the salty water down my cheeks.

Through my tears, I see that Hamid's eyes are boring into Mother's. What are his eyes saying? It is as if only the two of them are in the room.

Mother says, "The Qur'an says to not take life — which God has made sacred — except for just cause. Your father said that Muslims fight a just cause when they don't have the freedom to practice Islam, and when they are persecuted and oppressed by war."

"But Mother, Islamic Jihad *are* fighting a war," Hamid says.

"No! Islamic Jihad are reckless zealots."

"They are not. It's just that they've turned their backs on the hollow patriotism of the PLO, which has given us nothing. Nothing. Islamic Jihad are willing to act, not wait around for someone else to do something."

Mother makes a sound as if she is trying to catch her voice.

Hend says, "'Hollow patriotism of the PLO'? You sound as if you are quoting the Jihad. Have you been standing at some mosque while a radical *imam* is speaking? Are you passing out their handbills, Hamid?"

Hamid puts a hand up toward Hend, as if he is tired of her interruptions, and I see there is a blaze in his eyes. I squeeze my eyes shut. I don't want to see this. "No, I'm not passing out their handbills," he says.

"I hope not," Hend says. "Siftawi was convicted of murdering two Israelis and one Israeli Arab."

Mother pushes away from the table and stands up. "They stir up hatred. I do not want to hear any more talk of this." She pauses for a minute. "They are extremists."

Hamid jumps up. "Terrorism may be the only weapon for people who have no army."

I picture my father's eyes as he looked up from reading a newspaper story about a killing in Ireland. I was six. I hear Father's words in my mind, so clear: "Terrorism is like a wild dog. It only breeds violence."

Mother turns and looks at me, and then she looks back at Hamid. Her voice hardens. "No more talk, Hamid."

She holds out her right hand palm downward. She moves her hand up and down slowly. Her hand is saying *Be quiet*. I think she is too angry to speak.

Hamid answers with his hand. He holds his right hand out, palm downward, and then he jerks his hand, twisting his palm upward. *What? What?*

He lowers his face. Then he turns and looks at me. There is a burn in his eyes. This burn scares me. I fear it goes all the way down to his soul. He mouths the words *Jihad, now.* He has always shared his secrets with me. I have always kept them safe. But this secret does not feel safe. What will this secret do to him?

I do not think he will be content to be one of the *shabab* forever. *Jihad.* I feel a shiver course through my body. I get up from the table and leave the room. I hear Mother say, "Let her go," as I climb to the roof. Then she says, "And you, Hamid. You stay where you are. I have more to say to you."

RULA

ھ

Mother shakes me awake the next morning.
Hend is not in our bedroom. She is up already
or she slept in Mother's room again. "School,"
Mother says.

On the way to school, I notice that the Arafat
poster we saw two days ago is gone. Hamid is
quiet. At school, I don't look at Suhara. She does
not deserve even a look. I look at the girl sitting
on the other side of me. I don't recognize her;
she must be new. I wonder what her name is.
She wears a *hijab*. It is sitting crooked on her
head. It slips all the way onto her shoulders as she
writes. I can see her broad cheekbones, red, red
lips, and tiny pointed chin. She looks like she is
always cheery.

"Class, it is time for reading," the teacher says. "Open your books to the second chapter. Rula, I would like you to read for us. Start at the top of page ten."

The new girl sitting next to me begins to read. She reads one word at a time. She reads slowly. Near the end of the page, she stops at a long word, *obligation*. I whisper it to her, and she says it and finishes reading the page. Her brown eyes meet mine. *Thanks,* they say.

I get a knowing quiver inside me. This means something good is going to happen. Rula and I will be friends. I'm sure of it. I smile back.

In the afternoon, during geography, the teacher asks for the name of the country that has the most people living in it. I surprise everyone when I raise my hand. "China," I answer. *You are smart,* I say to myself.

I look over at Rula. I stare at her until she looks up, and then I lift my eyebrows, pull up the corners of my mouth just the tiniest bit, and let my eyes say, *Can we be friends?* I'm sure she gets their meaning. I turn away.

After school, Hamid meets me at the door. He hands me a giant pink hibiscus. He must have gotten it from someone's garden. Rula comes out, and I tell Hamid that she is my friend.

"Wait one minute," he says. He darts out of the schoolyard. We stand and wait a few minutes.

Rula says, "Does he always do things like this?" I just nod and smile as Hamid walks back into the schoolyard with his hand behind his back.

"Peace be upon you," he tells us and gives a little bow of the head. "And this one is for you," he says as he hands Rula a big red hibiscus. She giggles and looks down.

Rula and I walk together along the sandy street. Hamid is across from us, and when I look over, I see that the thick cords of telephone wires are dangling down from one side of a telephone pole. On the other side of the pole, a pair of old shoes and a Palestinian flag are looped over the wires. Getting that flag down will be a job for someone. The soldiers will make someone from the street take it down.

"I do not like Suhara," Rula says. "She just talks and talks, going on and on. She sounds like a buzzing bee. Buzz, buzzing."

"More like an annoying fly," I say. "I'd like to swat her."

Rula says, "This is the street my aunt lives on. She is a teacher." As she points, I see that another Arafat poster is back up on yet another wall. "My mother and I moved in with her because my mother is sick and my father is in prison."

Her words catch my breath. She puts her hand in her pocket and pulls out a piece of paper folded into many small squares.

"The lawyer who sees my father brought this to my mother, and she gave it to me." Very carefully she unfolds the paper and smoothes it out. She begins to read, one word at a time. "'Dear Rula, I miss you very much. Take good care of your mother for me. If God wills, I will be home soon. Your father.'"

Tears slip down my cheeks as she reads. I quickly brush them off before Rula can see them.

"I will see you tomorrow, Malaak."

Questions are crowding me and I can't talk. I nod and touch her arm. She turns down her street. I continue to walk toward our house, but my mind is full of letters. My father has been in prison for six weeks. Why didn't I get a letter from him? Why doesn't Mother talk of lawyers? She must not think he is in prison. But where is he, then?

Hamid shouts from across the street. He waves at me and then stoops to watch the old men playing cards under the stone archway.

When I look back at my side of the street, I see two women. One has a basket on her head. They are looking at me. I know them; they live next to each other at the end of our street. From the way they are staring, I can tell they are talking about me. They turn away. The one with the basket takes it off her head and holds it. Soon they lean toward each other. Why were they watching me? I step behind a tall man wearing a black-and-white *keffiyeh* and a long robe. I follow him until I am close to the women. Then I duck into an alley next to them. It is a narrow walkway. Old stone walls are on either side of me. And there, blooming in the crumbling stone at the base of the wall, is a tiny white flower.

"Poor little girl. Her father's been gone for six weeks now. They say she waits on the roof. Staring after him."

"She's hardly talked since then either."

"Yes, I know."

"I think they closed the border on the day he left. It was closed for a couple of weeks. That's longer than usual. I think there was some sort of bombing incident." Their voices are growing faint. They are moving away.

A couple of weeks? After a bad incident, the Israelis usually punish all of Gaza by closing the border to Israel and not allowing people to go to work there for a few days. But when they close it for a long time, it has to be some sort of awful incident. I see the word *bombing* in my mind. Bright light in the dark. It is flashing over and over. Then white light is filling my head, pressing my eyes.

I hear Hamid calling to me, "Malaak, Malaak."

I'd sunk down without realizing it. When I stand up, I reach for the wall to steady myself. And then I see the tiny crushed flower.

Hamid peers into the walkway. "Malaak, come here." He grabs my arm. "Why did you keep walking? You know I am supposed to watch for you. You saw me stop. You should have waited. You frightened me, Malaak. Don't do that again. Please." The word *please* is as soft as a whisper.

"Okay," I say to him. "Did Mother ever get a letter from the prison?"

"Not that I know of. Why do you ask that?"

"Rula did," I say. Hamid looks at me but says nothing. He shakes his head and holds on to my arm until we are home.

When we get there, he says, "You stay here; I'll be back soon. I have some things to do." I wonder where he is going. I remember the burn in his eyes when he said *Jihad.* Is he listening to more of Nasser's stories? At least they only tell stories to one another. But what if Hamid is making up his own stories in his head now? *Oh, Hamid, please.*

Hend is not home. Mother is at work as usual. I wonder where Hend is.

I go to the roof and Abdo flies to my shoulder. My thoughts circle round and round. They remind me of a yellow dog I saw on my street once. The dog was chasing its tail. When the dog caught his tail, he bit it and yelped. One thought catches another and bites it. *Yes, my father's been gone a long time. No, we haven't heard from him, but that's because he's in prison, right? Prisoners don't talk, right? But prisoners do talk. They send letters. But Hamid said we didn't get a letter.* I am so tired. I go back down to my room and fall across my mattress.

A word yelps me awake, just as I'm dropping off to sleep. *Bombing. Bombing.* Then the word *Father.* A shaft of pain shoots through my chest and squeezes my shoulders. *What if he isn't in prison? What if he is dead? Or missing like the man down the street? The man who is nothing?*

The tight dark pulls my mind into its hug, pressing the thoughts right out of it. Screaming startles me. I suddenly realize I'm the one who is screaming. I can't stop.

A door slams somewhere, and then my mother is there, with Hend behind her. Mother grabs me and holds me tight.

"I must know. I must know something. Tell me. Why do we never hear from Father?" I sob into her shoulder. "Why doesn't he send letters from prison like Rula's father does?"

"Why do you think your father is in prison, Malaak?"

"I know he is in prison. He has to be. I see him when I fly in Abdo's eyes."

"Oh," she says. Then she is quiet for a long time. She rocks me for a while. My eyes are closing.

FATHER

∽

I wake up with a blurry head. As I walk to the kitchen, I see that Hend and Mother are cleaning. I look at the clock and realize that I am late for school, and I wonder why Mother hasn't left for work yet.

"Why didn't you wake me? I missed the rooster." I smile at the groggy sound of my voice.

"You needed to sleep, Malaak, and I need to talk to you this morning. You said that you must know something. You are right. Knowing something is better than knowing nothing. So I will tell you what I know."

I sit down at the table.

"You said that you see your father, and I know

you see him. But he is not in prison. I believe he is in Paradise, with God."

A roaring fills my ears. I tear my eyes from her. *Paradise*. I fight the dark. *No*.

"Look at me, Malaak." Mother's eyes pull me out. "Do you remember he was going to look for a job in Israel? He was going to the border, to get a bus into Israel. In the evening, he would return. That afternoon, while I was cooking in the kitchen, I felt something touch my shoulder. It was like your father used to do when he snuck up from behind to surprise me. I turned but there was nothing there. Only the face of your father in my mind. Image after image of him flowed through me: the first time I saw him at my cousin's wedding, when he first met my parents and we had tea, and when he first saw Hend. She let out quite a cry, and he jumped. The first time he held Hamid's tiny fist, and his smile was so wide a bird could fly in. And you, Malaak, you never walked. You lurched forward into his arms like you couldn't wait to run. Our last picnic at the beach, do you remember it?"

I nod.

"So clear, each image, as if I were seeing a movie. Finally, that last picture, Malaak, of his green shirt, the one he was wearing the day he left. I was watching him from the front door as he called to you and gave you the I-am-winning sign before he turned the last corner. I knew that something had happened."

Hend squeezed Mother's hand.

"I waited and waited but no one came. That night, Hend and I carried you downstairs and put you to bed. The next afternoon, when he still wasn't home, I went to the market and heard people talking of a terrible incident. Something with a bus. But no one knew anything for sure. Finally, I went home. That night I told you he was missing."

"Mother," Hend says, but Mother just keeps talking in singsong. The tears flow down her face.

"The next day I saw a paper. On the front was a picture of a bus in two pieces. It was twisted and black. It was on the road to Jerusalem. There were mostly Israelis aboard, but a few Palestinians were also going to work. While I was standing there in the market, I read the article. It said there was only one survivor. A boy who was not expected to live long. The paper said that the bus had broken down, and someone in a passing car had seen an Arab man get off the bus to help the driver fix it. Another man got off and started running away. A minute later a bomb went off. Islamic Jihad claimed responsibility. A victory in their war with Israel. Then I knew the meaning of the touch on my shoulder. Your father was the Arab mechanic."

My mother turned and looked at Hend. "Hend, would you make us some bitter coffee?" Hend went to the kitchen to make the coffee that we drink when we are in mourning.

"Your father's ID papers were in his clothes. Gone with the rest of him. I knew the name of the mechanic, but no one else did, and I could prove nothing. But it was the right time of day, the right bus. Malaak, if your father were alive, he would have found a way to tell us. He loved us too much. Some women still come to me and say,

'Have hope, Ibtisam.' They don't know what I know in here." She places her hand on her chest.

"Do you remember that night when I told you he should be home by now and that he was missing?" I nod. "All I knew that night was that he was missing, but later on, when I was sure in my heart, I was afraid to tell you. You had stopped talking. I told Hend, and then I told Hamid after he talked about Islamic Jihad. I hope it will keep him from admiring them. You've spoken so little for six weeks now. What could I say to you, Malaak? I didn't realize that you thought he was in prison. You began to live in the little world of the bird and the roof. I was afraid for you, Malaak. I wanted to protect you somehow." My eyes are in her eyes, drowning in the Dead Sea.

"Come, Malaak, take my hand." She pulls me up, and I follow her to the roof. She leads me to our spot. "You have always had one hand in Heaven, and one on Earth. Even the birds talk to you, Malaak. You are your father's angel here on Earth." She stands behind me. "Look, Malaak." I know she is looking at the place where he said goodbye to us. I look too, and then I know. I see the green shirt, the backward glance, the I-am-winning sign.

He isn't coming back. My palms sweat. I feel the dark. It is trying to squeeze me, but it is fighting with something else in me. It is tears.

"No, no more dark," I whisper.

The tears come from deep inside of me. My mother holds me. "Yes, yes," she whispers. She is crying too. I cry until I can't.

"There is no strength or power except through God." She says it over and over, as she strokes my hair. Finally, we walk downstairs to the kitchen. Mother, Hend, and I drink the bitter coffee of mourning. I taste the bitterness all the way down to my soul. I feel the bitterness all the way down to my soul.

POEMS

∽

The next morning, when I roll over, there is such a tiredness in my brain. My eyes feel swollen. I shake my head to get rid of the tiredness. Then I remember that my father is dead.

As I put on each piece of clothing, I say the words "Father is dead." With each bite of food, I say them. Pretty soon I'm saying them so fast, they don't even sound like real words, just a slur. They don't make sense anymore. I can't hear them.

I climb to the roof and sit with Abdo. The words come back. *Father is dead.* They try to pull me into the silent darkness again as I feel the sadness. "You have no power over me," I whisper to them.

All through the day, whenever the sadness comes, I pinch my arm to make the sadness go there. That takes it out of my heart. When I go to bed that night, I see a bruise on my arm.

"Malaak, do you want to go to school?" my mother calls in the morning. This day comes with yesterday's tired feeling, so I say the words to myself again. "You have no power over me." But I pinch the other arm. Then I yell, "Yes!" downstairs to my mother.

I get out of bed, thinking of school and Rula. I missed two days this week. Yes, I want to see Rula.

When I go downstairs, Mother is dressed in black.

She sees me looking at the black clothes. "Yes, Malaak. I am in mourning now. I will show the world that what I know in here"—she points to her heart—"is true."

It has been two weeks since the street barricade and fighting, but the windows up and down our street are still shuttered, with bars across them. So many closed eyes. The doors of the houses are also closed tight. So many closed mouths. But one faded green door is splintered. Kicked in by soldiers' boots.

At school, the teacher says, "It is time to work on writing. Get out the words that you looked up in the dictionary." Rula reads out loud when the teacher calls on her. "'The desert is an arid region. It has little vegetation. There are few forms of life because there is little water.'" It sounds like sentences and not just words. I'm surprised. Rula must be practicing her reading at home. I look at her and she grins.

"Very good, Rula. Class, what is in the desert?"

Suhara lifts her hand. The teacher calls on her. "Sand," she says with a smirk.

"Well, yes. Anything else, Suhara?"

"Camels and Bedouins." Again Suhara smirks. She thinks she is so clever.

"We are so familiar with the desert that we don't really think about it anymore," the teacher says. "I want us to think in unfamiliar ways. This will help us to write better. What else is in the desert?" The teacher looks around for other answers.

Another girl, Fadwa, lifts her hand. "Oil, if you are in Saudi Arabia." Everyone else laughs.

Even the teacher smiles, but then she goes on. "What is something that looks like it exists in the desert but may not be real?"

Everyone is quiet. I look at the teacher, but she is staring out the window. Her forehead is crinkled, and her finger taps the desk. Finally, she says, "I will read a definition and you must guess what this is. 'Something unreal or without substance. An optical event that makes reflected or distant objects appear inverted. This occurs when the air closer to the ground is denser than the air above.'"

I shoot my hand up. *"Mirage,"* I say when she calls on me. I look over at Suhara, but she pretends that she didn't even hear me, and she turns and talks to her friend.

"Buzz, buzz, buzz," Rula says.

I whack my hand on the desk, and we giggle until the teacher stares right at us.

"Let's listen to these lines from a poem by

Ahmad Muhammad al Khalifa. The poem is called 'The Lost Mirage.'

> *"'O Mirage, do you not complain of*
> *weariness at noonday heat?*
> *You appear like water on the vast horizon,*
> *goading the traveler to lengthen out his way.'"*

She stops, and the room fills with the desert. I feel my tongue swelling with thirst.

"Now each of you must write a four-line poem about the desert. Oh, and you can't use the words *sand, camel, Bedouin,* or *oil.*"

I rest my head in my hands as I think. I wish that I could write like Hamid. I write my poem, and then we move on to mathematics.

Hamid is waiting for me after school. He has a large plastic container in one hand and two smaller jugs in the other.

"Here," he says, and hands me the smaller jugs. "We must walk to the gas station and get some water. It has been shut off again, and Mother is afraid we will run out."

I move my head back and raise my eyebrows. This means "no." Hamid stares at me. I move my chin upward and click with my tongue. This *really* means "no." Still Hamid stares, but now his mouth is hanging open.

"We will walk Rula home first," I tell him.

He starts and blinks. "Okay," he says. I realize he has forgotten that I used to tell him what to do now and then. He got used to my quiet. I give him a wide grin and turn sharply to start walking with Rula, barely missing the ficus tree that grows in front of the school. The leaves of the ficus are drooping and withered.

"Look at the leaves," I say to Rula. I pat the tree; it looks so sick.

Rula says, "It's the tear gas. It kills little children and old people too. The women's committee in the village where we used to live discussed it. They told women to keep fresh onions handy. People were to sniff them when tear gas came. My mother always took an onion when we went outside. Ugh! When I think of my village, I think of the smell of onions." She wrinkles her nose.

As we walk toward Rula's house, I tell her about my father. As I say each word out loud, it is made real. Talking sends the truth deeper inside me, moving through the wordless place that still seeks to pull me in at times. I step on a patch of pale grass at the edge of the street. It grows in a large crack between the road and the building. Rula steps on it also. The grass is like the tree, wispy and withered before it should be. Old, not young.

Rula has no words for me, but I see oldness in her eyes too. It is good to share this sadness with her.

When we are almost at Rula's house, she turns and says, "Tomorrow, Malaak. I will see you tomorrow."

Hamid and I trudge on to the gas station. I try to avoid a pothole but nearly get run down by a dented blue Peugeot. The air is dusty and so hot that I want to stop, but I don't. It is worse to be without water. Once, the water was shut off for two weeks in the al-Bureij refugee camp south of Gaza City. Water shutoffs are another way that the Israeli government gets back at people.

"Do you know why the water was shut off?" I ask Hamid.

"No," he says. Lots of times you don't. But many small children get very sick with diarrhea when there is no water. Now Mother sends us for water at the first hint of a shutoff.

"I do not want to spend my life standing in lines," Hamid grumbles as we stand there. "Lines for water, lines to get buses to cross the border, lines to go through checkpoints just because you are a Palestinian. Laughing lines, where the soldiers make fun of you. Lines to be searched — stripped naked and searched for bombs. It happened to me, Malaak, when I went with Father to visit our uncle. It could happen to you. They even do it to five-year-old girls."

The thought makes me feel sick, and I am already tired and thirsty. "I do not want to hear any more," I say to him. I just stare across the road and see a little boy eating an orange.

Once, at the beginning of the intifada, Hamid stole two oranges from an orchard. We were on the road going south to the Khan Yunis refugee camp, to see some distant cousins, but there were lots of cars at the Kfar Daron checkpoint. The taxi driver turned around and headed down a potholed one-lane path for cars. There were orange trees and cactuses around us. Then our taxi broke down, and Father and the driver got out to fix it.

It was night, and Hamid let me go only a little way from the taxi. Then he told me to be on the lookout. The stars were clear and sharp. I counted them as I waited and looked. Hamid was quick. The stolen oranges were delicious. We ripped off the peels and ate the fruit so fast, the juice ran down our chins. I shivered with fear and sweetness. That was a long time ago.

Today, there is just the dust swirling in the air. It makes me think of my poem.

"Have you ever seen a mirage?" I ask Hamid.

"Once," he answered. "It looked like a river splitting the desert and the sky."

"I see a mirage," I say.

"The air is not dense enough, Malaak. I do remember that from school."

"It is dense to me. I can hardly breathe. And I do see a mirage. Listen to this:

"I see a man walking.
He is wet from the desert river.
He lifts his callused hand to me.
And with this hand, he shakes the air."

Hamid looks where I am looking. "I wish I could see that mirage, Malaak. But I can't. But your poem is good. Better than any I used to write."

I do not want this to be a poem, or a mirage. I want it to be real. I want my father to wave his hand and shake the air once again.

I stare so hard that I am dizzy. But there is no mirage. Only heat rising from dust. I turn from the road and concentrate on counting the people in line ahead of us. Finally, we are at the tap and I fill the jugs. I am so tired when we get home that I just go inside and lie on the old sofa. Then I climb the stairs to the roof to say good night to Abdo. *Do you see the mirages, Abdo?* Abdo tilts his head. *Yes, you do. You see more than people do.*

TARIQ

∾

"Malaak, get up," says my mother. When I come down for breakfast, she is already in the kitchen. She is there before me most of the time. She says prayers and then makes breakfast. As I stand by the tiny table in the kitchen where she works, I hear the *drip, drip* of the kitchen tap. I go to kiss her cheek, and there are tears on it. One drips into the sink.

I have been at school every day for two weeks now. Rula and I walk home together every day, with Hamid of course. To school, home from school, each day, same thing. As if nothing had ever happened. As if sadness only lived at the edge of our lives instead of in the middle.

But then there are the nights. Mother says to me each evening, "There is tomorrow, Malaak. With God's help, we will take one step and one step."

I must get through each night filled with the figures that flash in the corners of my room. When I close my eyes, I see them behind my eyelids. Red graffiti, crushed white flowers, wispy yellow grass, smoky mirages. And then I picture Father. His upraised hand, his ocean hands, his worker hands. And I remember Mother's words, only I change them a bit. *Bravery is not seen in one act. It is measured by the choices in the night. The choices behind the eyes. Bravery is not seen in one act. It is measured by the choices in the night.* I say this over and over until I fall asleep.

Only in the morning can I take one step and one step. There is always the night first.

After breakfast, I wander into the living room and drop onto a chair. Hend has a radio playing in the bedroom, and the music floats down to me. Then it stops, and the announcer says that there is a general strike today. All the shops are closed, and children won't go to school. Gaza is mourning. It is the one-year anniversary of the death of a political prisoner.

Mother comes out of the kitchen and says, "Here is a list of chores for you to do today. Because of the strike, I won't go to work until this afternoon. Right now, I'm going to start things going for our dinner."

Tariq opens the front door without knocking and says, "Where is Hamid?" I reply with a shrug. I see that his smile does not reach his eyes. His right hand flurries toward his hair, touches his *taqiya,* and then settles on his shoulder. After a minute it flutters down to his pocket and finally rests on his other hand.

Why does he always wear that hat? Every day he wears it. For as long as I've known him, he has worn it, and he's always been around. He's been Hamid's best friend since they were little.

"I haven't seen him, Tariq," my mother says, coming into the living room. "Here, would you like a sweet?" She is always giving things away.

Even to wounded stray dogs like Tariq. He eats more at our home than he does at his own. He has no brothers or sisters, and he is really poor. His mother is probably glad to share Tariq with us.

His eyes shoot to the floor, and he walks quietly in. There is a grayness in him. I haven't really looked at him much before, but now I can see that it starts in his eyes and spreads out all around him. Tariq gobbles the sweet, then leaves.

We both stare after Tariq for a time. "Tariq reminds me of a wounded animal," I say.

"He is wounded, I do know that. Something hurt him badly. He doesn't say much, does he?" Mother says. "But then, I guess you know about that."

"Yes." Until Father died, I hadn't known what it meant to be wounded into silence, but now I do. And now I can see it in others. It's like the first time I lost a tooth. Before that I never noticed missing teeth, but after I lost mine, I saw gaptoothed people everywhere.

"I believe that Tariq has a place where words don't live. It is deep inside of him," Mother says.

She turns toward me and tilts her head. This is her weighing look. She is weighing her words like the man weighs the fruit in the market. Then she goes back into the kitchen. I follow her. She picks up her knife and moves toward the table where the vegetables are. I step in front of her. She stops, and her knife hand drops to her side.

"Tell me what happened to Tariq." I stare into her eyes, and they widen.

Mother squares her shoulders and speaks slowly. "You are learning so many things at one time. I know you are seeing people differently now, but still some things are hard for me to tell you, Malaak. I wish that Tariq could tell you this story, but I don't think he can. He is living in the quiet, so I will tell you his story."

She takes a deep breath and begins. "When Tariq was little, his father was shot by Israeli soldiers. Tariq was with his father. He carried a piece of his father's shirt home with him. It was still in his hand when he went to bed that night. His mother said he cried and moaned all that first night, saying, 'The pieces, the pieces.' The *taqiya* he wears was his father's. When his father was shot, part of Tariq was lost. He looks for it. He looks in Hamid and in many other places. Everywhere and anywhere."

The fluorescent bulb on the ceiling sends out a greenish hue. It blinks off and on again. "Would you like to help me with the meal, Malaak?" my mother asks. I don't want to cook, but I do not want to leave the steamy kitchen. Or to stop watching my mother do what she always does.

"Here." She hands me the big spoon. "Stir the garlic."

I watch my hand scraping and turning. The smell of roasting garlic gets strong, and I hear the *plonk, plonk, plonk* of my mother's knife. Then she pours sauce into my pan, and I start stirring.

"We are having *mahshi*," she says. *Mahshi* is one of my favorite meals. Mother fills onions, squash, and peppers with rice. I don't like stuffing vegetables. Stirring is better, but it makes me hungry.

"Please keep stirring carefully, Malaak. Be sure to scrape the bottom of the pan. You don't want it to burn there. You will cook as well as I do if you keep listening and paying attention to me." My mother wants the sauce cooked very slowly. Simmering. She believes in the traditional cooking. She is good at it. Sometimes she cooks holiday meals for the rich women she cleans for.

As I stir, Mother's words sink into the sauce. *Tariq's father. My father.* They join together and go round and round like my hand. My mother leaves the kitchen.

That night, at supper, there is a knock. Tariq has returned. "Come in, Tariq," my mother says. "Wait here for Hamid." Soon Hamid comes in and we all sit down to eat. I watch Tariq. While he is eating, a smile flicks his mouth, but it does not touch his eyes.

Hamid and Tariq watch television. It is an old American movie. I join them, but Hend helps Mother in the kitchen. When I look at Tariq, I think of his father. His father is in a wordless place, and it seems that Tariq has gone there to find him. My father is in a wordless place too. Sometimes I still feel the pull to go there and be with him. Live with him. But the pull does not happen as much as it used to.

Tariq does not speak the whole evening. But that is not unusual for him.

We hear the blaring of a bullhorn. Even though we can't distinguish the words too well, we know that it is a soldier announcing the curfew. When the Israeli authorities heard about the general strike, they announced a new curfew. "Hurry home, Tariq. You should have left earlier," my mother says. "I don't want you to be picked up and arrested just for being in the street at the wrong time. I hope this curfew doesn't last as long as the last one."

"I heard that in Jabalia camp, where the intifada started, the curfew has been every night since the beginning," Hend says.

"Before you know it," Hamid says, "curfews won't be only in the evenings. They will be all day too. Then we'll just call it what it really is: house arrest. That's what it feels like."

Tariq runs outside. My mother bolts the windows and doors. We hear the soldiers go by.

I climb to the roof and watch Tariq as he walks home. I am afraid for him. He could be picked up just for crossing the street. He doesn't need any more bad things. Especially with soldiers. Abdo watches with me. *Look into the darkness, Abdo. Look ahead of him, of me. Can you warn us of danger? Can you see it?*

THE WARNING

⌒⌒

Two days later the strike is over. After I get home from school, I go to the roof to feed Abdo. Abdo doesn't eat. He scratches my hand, scattering the seeds, and flies to the edge of the roof. I look down into the street and see Hamid. He and Tariq are standing on the corner. It looks like they are watching for soldiers. This stupid *shabab* stuff could get them beaten. I do not want anyone in my family to get hurt. My eyes focus tightly on them. Hamid and Tariq wait until they see a soldier, and then whistle and yell. *Stupid. Stupid.*

They turn and run back a little way into our street, and the soldier turns toward them. My mind explodes. The heat shoots through my arms and goes into my hands. I pound my fist into my palm as Tariq and Hamid each bend down to pick up something off the street. I am sure it is stones. "You fool, Hamid! Will you get killed too?" I scream from the roof. I run downstairs and into the sitting room. Hend is running to the front door.

I hear a deep voice shouting. I follow Hend through the doorway and then bump into her as she stops dead. Looking around her, I see that my mother is outside running toward the end of the street where a soldier is shouting. He is saying, "Go home! Go home! Get out of the street!"

"Help, help," I whisper, pressing my knuckles into my cheeks. Hamid and Tariq have stopped. Their arms are stuck out in front of them.

My mother drops to her knees with a loud cry. The soldier looks down at my mother and says something to her, but I can't hear it. My body is poised. I'm on tiptoe with my calves flexed tight.

My mother raises her face to him. Then the soldier raises his rifle into the air and shoots it straight up. Hend screams.

Tariq and Hamid move instantly. They run to the alley behind our house. An Israeli jeep rounds the corner, but the soldier on the street yells in Hebrew. He motions to the driver to move on, and the jeep roars away. The soldier turns and walks to the end of the block. My muscles droop, and relief soaks me. Sweat rolls down my face and under my arms.

My mother does not move. She is still on her knees. Her shoulders are shaking. My legs are wobbly, and I slowly make my way to her. Hend is ahead of me. Soon I join them.

"What did he say to you, Mother?" I ask.

"He said, 'I have two sons,'" my mother replies in a shaky voice.

"And did you say something back to him?" Hend asks.

"I said, 'May God keep you safe then.'" None of us moves.

Silence flutters down on us. It feels like Abdo lighting on my shoulder. This is safe. This slight moment, this space of rest, feels larger than now.

Could *safe* go on and on? I want it to. *Oh, yes,* I pray. *Go on forever.*

Later, when Hamid comes inside, my mother says, "I do not want you to act like one of the *shabab*. You might only yell or throw stones, but the soldiers could beat you or arrest you. I've lost my husband. I will not lose my only son."

Hamid says, "I would have been fine. Those soldiers wouldn't have done anything."

"You do not know that, Hamid."

"You won't lose me, Mother. But I have to be a part of the cause. Father shouldn't have lost his job because of the intifada. He shouldn't have had to go to Jerusalem to look for another job. There shouldn't have to be an intifada in the first place." I hear something different in Hamid. He's not just saying what someone else has said.

"Father believed in a Palestinian land. He wanted the Palestinians to have the same things the Israelis do — jobs, land, water. You think I am just a boy, but I am not anymore."

My mother begins to cry. I think she hears the change in Hamid. She goes upstairs.

I used to say that Hamid's fist was in his mouth, because he was more big talk than actual fighting. Now his hand will be his fist. He has become a stone fighter.

Hamid turns the television on to a soccer match and slouches on the sofa. I sit beside him. He frowns at the TV as he watches. He falls asleep sitting up. I turn the TV off and go to bed.

It is after school the next day, and I am sitting at the table. I am drawing roses that are in a vase on the table. Only, in my picture the roses are real, not plastic. Hend is watching her soap opera. Hamid sits down beside me and watches me. Hend's show ends and she goes upstairs. I hear the *whack, whack* of a knife in the kitchen, Hend's radio upstairs, and a yell from the street all at the same time. Each noise is clear, sharp. Each sound is much too loud.

The front door opens and Tariq rushes in. "Nasser has been beaten. It was in the next street over." My mother hurries out from the kitchen.

Hamid jumps up. He and Tariq rush outside. In ten minutes they are back, and Hamid says, "Nasser was on his way home from school. He went into a store to buy some food. While he was there, someone must have thrown a stone. When he came out of the store, the Israeli patrol grabbed him and beat him with truncheons. A woman saw the whole thing and knew he had done nothing. She tried to stop the blood flow, but the soldiers wouldn't let her."

"Oh no!" my mother says. "Hamid, come. We must find out how he is doing." I turn to climb the stairs to the roof; I want to get away from the news. I want to be up in a safe place—a place where there are no words to tell of horrible things.

When I am on the roof, Abdo flies to my hand. We both look down on Mother and Hamid as they leave the house. Mother stops at a small group of women, and I see them talking together. But Hamid darts ahead, rounds the corner of the street, and then I can't see him anymore. Even though it is hot on the roof, I feel a chill curving down through my insides. *What is he running into?*

Mother comes back after a few minutes. "Malaak, come down and eat," she calls up to me. "I didn't find out anything else, except that they are waiting for an ambulance."

"Where is Hamid?" I ask when I get downstairs. I sit on the sofa and stare across at the wall, at a little framed picture of our family — Father, Mother, Hend, Hamid, and me. We are all sitting on the sand, on a red blanket. There is food in front of us and an ocean behind. *Could that have been only two years ago?*

"I believe he is waiting for the ambulance," says Mother. "I'm sure he will be home soon." When I hear these words, the chill curves through me again and I know I can't eat. I go to my room and lie on the mattress. I find that I am curving around the chill inside, curving until I'm a little ball. I'm waiting for Hamid's voice.

Sometime later I hear Hend say, "You are late," and then I hear Hamid. At the sound of his voice, my legs stretch, and I jerk. Tiredness comes. I can't make out Hamid's words, he is talking so quietly. But it doesn't matter. He is home.

I wake up slowly and go downstairs. Even though it is morning, I'm not hungry for breakfast. I sit on the sofa and stare at the other picture on the wall. It is a picture of my mother's family. My mother's older sister is only two, and my grandfather is leaning down to pat her head. My mother is a baby, not yet one. My grandmother is holding her and squinting at the camera. My mother's younger sister is not born yet. The family is in a garden with jasmine trees and an olive tree. In the corner of the picture are very small handwritten words, which I do not need to read. *Jerusalem, 1946.*

My mother's family was from the town of Lydda. The Jewish soldiers drove thousands of Palestinians from their homes in Lydda in 1948. The British had evacuated Palestinians before, but then the British let people go back, so my grandparents thought the same thing would happen again. They just locked their house and left. My mother still has the key.

This picture on the wall was from a family visit to Jerusalem during happy times. The only ones in the family who are still alive are my mother and her younger sister, who isn't in the picture.

When I was little, I would close my eyes and pretend that I was in that beautiful place in Jerusalem and that nothing had changed since that picture. I would smell the jasmine. I would eat the olives.

The light catches the picture's gilded frame as Mother comes into the room. Her skin is stretched like fine paper. Her eyes are sunken. The lids look so dark, I almost think she has darkened them, but I know she hasn't. She looks like she didn't sleep at all last night.

She tells me that when Hamid got home, he said that Nasser had died before the ambulance reached the hospital. She puts her arms around me and hugs me. Even though I didn't know

Nasser that well, I begin to cry. My mother cries too. I do not know where my sadness starts or where her sadness starts. The sadness mingles with all the pain in the last months and flows down our faces.

THE FUNERAL

∽

The next day, I think about Nasser's funeral. But I find my mind jumping to Father's funeral instead. If Father had died like Nasser, there would have been a funeral for him. We would have prepared for it. And I find that I am preparing for it. All day long I'm preparing food, clothes, words, for the funeral that will not happen.

I think that Hend and Mother are preparing too. I see them wiping tears from their faces at different moments when they think I won't notice.

By the third day, the day of the funeral, I am numb, for I've already played out Father's funeral in my mind so many times. We get ready to go to the family's house. Mother and Hend put on gray *jilbabs,* and I put on a blue one. The coats are long and cover us. We look like all the other women mourners who are out in the street. We are all walking toward Nasser's house.

We turn the corner to Nasser's street, and I see a large white canopy tent stretched in front of the house. There are red and black streamers decorating the tent. These are two of the colors in the Palestinian flag. People have been arrested for even having red, black, green, or white at a funeral.

The men go to the tent, and I glance into it as we walk by. Hamid is sitting with the older men, who are drinking tea. A large banner made of brown paper is hung up on the back of the tent. In the center of the banner is Nasser's picture. The numbness leaves, and I tremble. I reach out, and Hend takes my hand.

She pulls me into the house, where the women are, and my mother talks to Nasser's mother and aunts. Hend speaks to his sisters, while I stand quietly beside her. Talking seems too hard.

I can't think of words. I see Nasser's face. That mouth, that bold mouth that told stories. Quiet now.

We go up to the roof and stand with the other women. They are telling stories about Nasser. Some are chanting, and some are ululating. The trilling sound feels deeper than words, and I join in. We do not stay long.

As we walk by the canopy, Hamid comes over to Mother. "Go without me. I will walk with the men."

"The soldiers may come to this procession as they have to others before," she says.

"I know," Hamid says. "They do not want Nasser to be seen as a martyr for the Palestinian cause."

"Please do not stay here long, Hamid. If they do not leave for the burial soon, you must come home. I am afraid that something will happen."

"So am I," Hend says. Hamid just nods and turns away. Is he listening to their fears? I can only look at him with eyes that say *Please, please, Hamid, stay alive.* But he will not even look at me, and then we leave. When we are home, I climb to the roof.

"Come, Abdo." Abdo flies to my hand, and I try to find Hamid as we watch the streets below. *Please. Please, Hamid.*

Soon we see the funeral procession. It is on the street that meets with ours. I gasp when I see a young man with his face half covered by a *keffiyeh* walk in front of the coffin, holding a Palestinian flag. I finally pick Hamid out from the crowd. He is walking behind the coffin. Nasser's brother, Mahmoud, is one of the ones carrying the coffin at the front. Nasser's father is old, but now he looks ancient. He shuffles along as if he is blind.

Abdo knows my feelings. The sorrow is pulling at me as I watch Nasser's father. I turn to look the other way, and I see soldiers approaching. They are coming toward the funeral. They yell at the mourners, and I see Mahmoud yell back. The young man with the flag lowers it. I hear shouts from the soldiers again. Mahmoud yells back again, and then I see the soldiers lift their rifles. I look for tear gas canisters, but there are none. The young man with the flag drops to the ground, and a moment later I hear a shot and see the coffin tilting forward. People are running. The darkness from inside pulls at me until my sight is blurred.

I sit down on the roof. The sound of wailing and yelling increases. The darkness squeezes tighter, circling, drawing me down inside. Back to the sure silence. But then Abdo startles up, warning me as he flies to the top of the antenna. He looks at me, and I hear one more shot. There is shouting in the house, and I pinch my arm fiercely and run downstairs into the light of the kitchen. I force out the words, "Soldiers, shooting."

"We thought we heard a shot," Hend says, and then runs outside into the street. She leaves the door open, and I see her looking up and down.

Mother yells, "Come back in here," at Hend, but Hend doesn't come back. Mother circles me with her arms. "Breathe," she says. "Breathe deeply." I am not sure if she is talking to me or to herself, but I do know that her arms are too tight. I push on her arms.

"Let me go," I say to her. She lets go, and we both fill our lungs.

Hend runs back inside. "Someone yelled down the street that Mahmoud was the one who was shot. He is dead."

Mother gasps. Hend runs over, and the three of us hug. Then Hend says, "I'm sure they will bury him right away because they are afraid the soldiers will take his body away, like soldiers often do."

"And Hamid will stay until it is over," Mother says. "God be with him." We sit huddled together on the sofa. We don't move or speak. I think we are all using our energy to keep our fears down inside. Only our bodies speak to one another. I feel the tremors in Hend's legs as they bump against mine. I tremble too, and then I pass my tremors on to Mother.

And so we sit. After an hour or two, I don't know how long, Hamid comes inside. "Nasser's brother, Mahmoud, was shot. He was carrying the coffin in the funeral march. He died too. He was buried in the clothes he was shot in. They are his martyr clothes. They went right to the cemetery. Mahmoud was placed in the grave with Nasser. The old men said the prayers and read the Qur'an," Hamid says. His voice is flat. This flatness scares me more than anything. These deaths have changed him. He turns and goes to bed. The rest of us follow.

In the morning, Hamid says that he is going to Nasser's house to be with the family. "Please don't," Hend whispers. "Think of her, Hamid. Think of Mother."

But he turns toward the door. "Leave me be," he says with steel in his voice. I hear it, and I see it in his eyes.

Mother must go to work, but Hend stays home with me. Now we sit and wait again. It is quiet. After a while, Hamid opens the door and slips in. He slumps to the floor and begins to tell us of the mourning. On his shirt he has pinned a picture of the dead boy, Mahmoud. He rocks back and forth, chanting, like he is reciting poetry.

"Today we celebrated the life of two martyrs. There were green, red, black, and white streamers draped in the room. The Palestinian flag hung on the wall. Pinned on the front was a poem for the martyr sons. A song of the resistance played on the cassette player. Nasser's father read that poem. When he was done, he said that he was no longer afraid, for he was dead inside. 'I have given my all,' he said. 'There is nothing more anyone can take.'"

"All of you could have been shot right there," Hend said. "With the flag, the talk of martyrs, the Palestinian colors."

"Should I be afraid, Hend?" The chanting voice is gone. The steel is back in Hamid's voice.

I can't listen to it anymore. I hear my brother and sister arguing as I climb to the roof. I want to be with Abdo. Abdo listens and does not argue.

RIMAL

∾

It is morning. But before the rooster has a chance to crow, I hear my mother's voice. Why is she waking me so early? Then I remember it is Ramadan, our holy month. I'd forgotten because of the funeral. Ramadan is a time for purification, so we fast from food and unkind words, from sunup to sundown. Older people do not smoke or drink alcohol either.

I hate being hungry, but I love *iftar* at night, when we break the fast. People often visit one another too. And I love the feast and celebration at the end of Ramadan.

The fasting during Ramadan is one of the five pillars of our faith. The other four are our creed the *shahada,* prayer, alms giving, and the *hajj*—a spiritual pilgrimage to Mecca.

Mother encourages us in the faith and wants us to follow her beliefs. But as my father used to say, it will be up to me to choose Islam. He'd quote the Qur'an: "There is no compulsion in religion."

"*Suhur,*" Mother yells. "Time to eat." The clock in the kitchen reads 4:15. A sleepy-eyed Hend stumbles in. We eat our boiled eggs, bread, and cheese slices. Then I stumble back into bed for a few more hours of sleep.

A *slap, slap* noise wakes me up again. It is the sound of bread being flattened. Mother has much baking to do. Hend is staying home from school to help her. Murmurs rise from the kitchen.

"Goodbye," I tell them as I leave for school with Hamid. School seems longer than usual. I guess it is because I am hungry.

On my way home from school, I smell orange blossoms. Then I smell oranges. Or I want to smell oranges. My head is whining and my stomach is growling. I am as hungry as a wild dog. No, it's more than that. I'm as hungry as the donkey that wouldn't budge in the market a few weeks ago.

When I'm near our house, Mother sticks her head out the door and yells, "Hurry along, Malaak. We are going to Rimal. I need your help." I run inside.

"We must run to the taxi station, Malaak. Help us." I rush into the kitchen and help Mother and Hend carry out trays of bread, *atayif,* and buttery cakes. They have been cooking all day. During Ramadan my mother bakes extra things to take along to the families she cleans for. These people live in Rimal, a richer quarter of the city. Mother says the families were landowners who lived in Gaza before the refugees came.

Mother usually walks to work, but today her employers are paying for us to take a taxi because we are bringing the food. We load the taxi full of pastries, and then we stuff ourselves in. We head off for Rimal.

Hend whispers, "Can you imagine living in your family home and tracing your family back hundreds of years? Everyone living in the same place?" Her eyes are round and glassy. I wonder why she is whispering, but then I feel it too—the awe of belonging.

I whisper back, "No, Hend. I can't." I think of the picture on our wall. Of Jerusalem. We turn onto Omar al-Moktar, the main street of the city. We pass al-Jundi, the Square of the Unknown Soldier. Such a funny name, I think, as if there is only one unknown soldier. All Palestinians are unknown soldiers. I see some people walking in the garden.

We drive by the palm trees, and the big houses with arches and verandas. I can see roses and lilies and gladiolas in the gardens. There are other flowers too, but I don't know their names. This seems farther away to me than just the other side of the city. It seems like another country.

But then we pass a half-finished villa, with holes where the windows should be. I point to it, and Mother says, "A lot of construction has stopped because of the intifada." Beside the half-finished villa is an empty lot, where a goat is munching on some garbage. And I know that it is not another country. Just a different part of the same one.

"Hamid says that here in Rimal the children throw chocolate sweets at the soldiers," Hend whispers.

I start giggling. "If anyone throws chocolates around me, I will fight the soldier for them, and I will win."

We stop at a villa surrounded by palm trees. I can smell jasmine before I get there. I see behind the villa the glint of the gold sun on the sea.

A girl who looks about Hend's age comes out and takes us to the back of the house. She is wearing a maroon dress with gold cord on the neck and sleeves, and a necklace with a large amber stone. She has four bangles on one arm, and two on the other. I wonder who she is. We carry in the food and arrange it on inlaid wooden platters. We carry it to the eating room and set it on large side tables. Crystal lights in the ceiling are glinting like the ocean. There are pictures on every wall. Large vases filled with red and pink roses are on the main table, which is surrounded by chairs with white-and-black mosaic tile backs and plushy seats.

When no one is looking, I sit on the chair at the head of the table. *What would it be like to eat here?* I think of our messy, noisy suppers — Hamid talking with his mouth full of falafel, and my loud laughter. Something about this room makes me feel I have to be very quiet. I don't think our family could eat here.

When we are finished, the girl in the maroon dress pays the taxi driver, and now I know that she actually lives in that house. Maybe she is the daughter. Did she throw chocolates at the soldiers? I can't wait to get home and eat.

At home I eat mounds of saffron rice, hummus, and tiny fried fish. I can't stop, but when I see the buttery cake that Mother has saved for our dessert, I'm too full to eat it. I hide a piece in my sleeve.

I slip up to the roof to see Abdo. I know Abdo will like the cake. When I open my hand, he pecks down some crumbs. "Would you like a chocolate too?" I ask him.

I hear the *muezzin* calling for prayer. As I go down the stairs, I hear Mother and Hend praying in the kitchen. And then I hear Hamid's voice. He is praying too.

THE MEETING

∽

Ramadan is over. There was an uneasy quietness in the house during the holy month. As if Hamid were waiting, giving us the month to rest. As I go upstairs to feed Abdo, I suck in lungfuls of the quiet.

"I'm thankful for this peaceful quiet," I say to Abdo. I look down to the street and see Hamid leave our house. It looks like he's heading for school, but we don't have school today because the schools are closed again. *Where is he going?* I think that he is a stone fighter, but does he want to be something more?

When I go downstairs, I find that Mother has gone to work. I follow Hend around as she goes about daily chores. She hands me a broom, and I try to sweep the kitchen. But my hands are restless, and they just scatter the dirt. I sweep the kitchen over and over.

The jitters in my body are too strong. I want to run, jump, scream, throw stones myself, but I'm not supposed to leave our house. So instead, I race up and down the stairs to the roof. When I'm too tired to run anymore, I climb to the roof, my safe place, to be with Abdo. Abdo, who stays in the same place and doesn't change. I stroke Abdo over and over until the twitches leave my hand.

At the end of the day, Hamid returns, but still he says nothing. "Tomorrow," I say that night to Abdo, "I will find out what Hamid is doing. I will follow him the next time he leaves."

In the morning, after Mother and Hend have gone to work, I hear the front door close. I hurry downstairs to follow Hamid. When I get to the street, I find that Abdo is there too. He is right behind Hamid. When I turn the corner, Abdo is gone and Hamid is even farther down the street. I run to keep Hamid in sight.

I smell that awful smell again. Burning rubber. The burning smell gets stronger and stronger. I see Tariq step out of a doorway and join Hamid. They turn a corner, and when I catch up, I see a group of men, and fire streaking into the sky.

There are two metal barrels on either end of a wooden platform. Beside them are burning tires. Flames and thick braids of black smoke curl upward. I see Hamid and Tariq standing at the back of the group. There is a tall young man standing beside Hamid. I have not seen him before. I step into a doorway across the street. They can't see me, but I can see them well. I spot Abdo sitting on top of a nearby building. Why has he stopped here? How can I catch him? Perhaps he is watching Hamid for me.

Men in black hoods are standing up front. A speaker goes onto the platform. He also has a black hood over his head. The smoke swirls up, and the fire jumps as he speaks. His words find me in my dark doorway.

"I take refuge with God from Satan, the accursed one. Think not of those who are slain in Allah's way as dead. Nay, they live, finding their sustenance in the presence of their lord. God Almighty has spoken truly!"

These sound like words from the Qur'an. It must be some sort of religious meeting.

I look at Hamid. He is eager. He eats these words. His mouth opens and shuts. He clenches and unclenches his fists.

"We will not dishonor our heroes, our martyrs, by forgetting them. We honor the martyrs today. They are willing to sacrifice their lives to free people from the occupation. There are people all over the world today who are fighting against oppressors. Some will die. Every revolution has its martyrs."

Tariq stands there, unmoving. He doesn't even blink. I wonder if he hears anything. Maybe he is part stone already. A stone for someone to pick up and throw at a soldier. Shivers run down me, but I'm not cold. I look around at the men. Are any in Islamic Jihad? Are any in Hamas? Is there a bomber?

"Those who have died light the fires of revolution," the speaker says as he points to the burning cans and tires.

Then the speaker picks up a rock and holds it up. He points to an Israeli flag on the building where Abdo is.

"We will not stop until the thieves who stole our land are gone." He throws the rock at the flag. Other men start throwing rocks too.

"Abdo!" I scream. I run toward the building. At my scream, Hamid turns toward me and stares. He tries to grab me, but I punch him and run around him. He stands there open-mouthed. The flag is ripped, and Abdo is gone. I run like I've never run before, and when I get home, I rush to the roof. Abdo is there. I grab him and squeeze him to my chest. Words pour out of my mouth as Abdo wriggles to get out of my grasp.

"Thank you, God. He is alive. Thank you, God. He is alive." I laugh and choke at the same time. After a while I just sit and hold Abdo. My heart finally slows, and then I think about the rally, the fires, and Hamid, and I feel the *pound-pound* rhythm in my chest speeding up again. What can I do about Hamid? I will speak to him in the morning, I decide, even though I am not sure what I will say.

TALK

∾

I get up early to feed Abdo, and when I look down, I see that Hamid is already leaving the house. "Hamid!" I yell, but my voice comes out shrill, too high. "Hamid," I try again, but this time my voice cracks.

I slip downstairs and run out the door. I know that I should not be walking alone, but Hamid will not take me with him, so I must continue to sneak around to follow him. He will be furious if he finds out.

First Hamid gets Tariq. They wind in and out of alleys. It isn't too long before they stop. A tall boy comes out of an empty concrete-block building. I know him. He was at the religious meeting. They go into the building with him. I listen beneath a window, but I hear only snatches of words. "Bomb" and "week." *What week? What bomb?* A door slams. I jump up and start running, hoping I can remember the way back.

When I get home, Hend says, "Where have you been? Out with Hamid?"

I nod.

"Where is he then?"

"Still out, but I knew it was getting late, so I came home."

"Mother has gone to work already. Hurry, get ready for school. I will walk with you, but then I have to go to work too."

It is the longest day of school. I fidget, and fume inside. The teacher scolds me because I am not listening. She is right. Finally, it is over and Hend meets me outside and walks me home. I don't want to talk to her about anything.

I bounce up and down on the sofa as I wait for Hamid to come in. "Sit still," Hend says. "I'm trying to watch my show."

"I can't," I say. "I'm filled with prickles."

I'm relieved to see Hamid come in for supper. After supper I whisper to him, "You. Come to the roof with me." He laughs. My teeth clench. I stare hard at him and whisper again, "Let's talk about the religious meeting."

I know he will follow. He does.

"I followed you again this morning," I say. "Why were you with the young man from the meeting? Is he going to bomb something? What are you going to do?"

"Stop following me." Hamid's words spit from his mouth.

"Father did not believe in terrorist acts, Hamid, and he was killed by Islamic Jihad."

"Yes, all right. But what about Nasser and Mahmoud? Israelis killed them. For no reason. No reason at all. Is that any different? Isn't that terrorism?" He grabs me by my shoulders. "Innocent people die in buses, at shops, and during funerals. Innocent people die in wars. The Israelis took our land in a war. They killed women and children too. We are in a war, fighting with the only weapons we have." His eyes are lit from inside.

I wriggle to get free. "Are you saying that Father wasn't right?"

Hamid goes on as if he hasn't heard me. "And if we don't win this war, what future do I have, Malaak?" I wriggle more, but his long arms hold me away from him. He is strong.

"Let go of me, Hamid."

Then he starts laughing and drops his hands. "Goat Girl. Will you butt me with your head next?" I rub my shoulders. I am mad at him.

"But you must honor our father's life." My voice breaks even though I don't want it to. "He was a good and brave man."

Hamid turns and stares out across the roofs. "Blessed be his memory. He was brave, Malaak. But look out there at the people in Gaza City. And then look farther, to the thousands and thousands squashed into the refugee camps." His eyes glitter again. Lines have hardened in his forehead.

"There are no jobs, no chances. I do not want to live like this for the rest of my life. I'm not saying that Father isn't right. I do not seek to dishonor our father, but is one way always right and another always wrong?"

His glittery eyes are set. Hard. When I say nothing, his breath comes out in a short burst. His neck tightens, and he makes a chopping motion with his right arm. "Why do I even bother telling you? You don't understand, Malaak. How can you? You are just a girl."

But these words bring hot blood to my neck, to my face. My voice rises to a high pitch. "Yes, yes. Just a girl." Then the anger jumps from my throat. "But does Islamic Jihad think about the people who die? Real fathers, mothers, and children die when someone sets off a bomb in a bus or a car. Does Islamic Jihad think about those who are left? No, no."

"There are widows and orphans in every war, Malaak. It is no different now." Hamid looks down and begins to push a stone with his foot. Then he looks up and says, "I'm warning you. Don't tell Mother, or else."

"Or else what, Hamid?" I yell as I run down the stairs.

I don't sleep well. I'm running away from a bus. Wherever I go, it follows me. Through the back alley, past my school, past the marketplace. All the streetlights are broken. There is no light. Only the bus's headlights on me. I'm lost. I'm tired. I can't run anymore, and I drop down on the ground. I look at the windshield. It is Hamid driving. A scream fills my throat. I wake with one hand on my throat and one hand pushing the dark. I'm wet with sweat.

THE FLAG

∾

"Malaak, are you awake?" It is morning and Hamid is shaking me. He will keep doing it until I open my eyes. I hear Mother and Hend. They are talking in the kitchen.

"What?" I say, annoyed.

"I brought you something," Hamid says. I roll over and see bright colors in his hand. Black, red, green, and white.

"Do you remember the time that Father and I traveled to see Uncle Ayad?"

"Yes," I say.

"Kufr Nameh is just a small village perched on a stony hill—"

"Yes, yes, I know," I interrupt. "With olive trees between the houses."

"But as I was going to say, they are not afraid there, Malaak. They were flying the Palestinian flags everywhere. Uncle Ayad lowered the flag from above his house while we were there. He gave it to Father."

I nod, impatient with him. "And Uncle's family cheered and shouted. I remember. You told me this before."

"This is that flag. Father gave it to me. I hid it." He stretches out his hands with the flag in them. "Here. It's for you. Take it." I take the flag. This flag was in my father's hands, his car-stained hands. He used to wash them before supper and hold them up for me to inspect. I always let him eat even though I could still see the grease lines and the darkened fingernails. This flag belonged to those hands. If only I could feel the warmth of those hands in this flag.

I look into Hamid's beggar eyes.

"Look at me, Malaak. I am a fighter. You know that. I must find my own way. I think this way will bring change."

"I want you to be safe, alive."

"We are in a war whether you want to be or not. Father, Nasser, and Mahmoud are all dead. And they were not in Islamic Jihad. What is *safe*? I don't think anyone is safe. Not anymore." His voice breaks, but after a moment he goes on.

"They stole our land. Did words and waiting get us our land back? For forty years no one listened. I don't think that Father's way of words and patience worked." He closes his eyes.

He has thought about this. He is living from the inside out. I see a tear sneak from under his eyelid.

I reach to take the tear that wobbles on his chin. Hamid misses Father too. I touch my cheek with the flag. This is the best gift my brother could give to me. Even more precious than his poems.

"The rally you saw me at and the meeting with the boy yesterday must be our secret," he says. "I am sad that you know. I didn't want any of you to know because it could bring you harm. The less you know, the better."

I nod. What he says sounds right.

"I'm worried that Mother might find out too, and I know she needs to hear it from me. I just can't say anything to her now. I do not wish to add to her sadness. There has been too much pain in our family lately, so I will wait for a better time. There will be a better time."

I hug the flag to my chest. It is Hamid's sign of the trust between us. "I'm not sure there will be a better time, and I am not changing my mind about Islamic Jihad. But for now, Hamid, I see that you are thinking of Mother. I will keep your secret, but it frightens me. Promise me you'll tell her soon."

"I will. Thank you, Malaak."

I hug Hamid, and when he leaves, I rub the softness of the flag into my neck.

DRIVING LESSONS

❧

At school, the teacher talks about mathematics, but I'm thinking about Hamid. *What if someone sees him at a meeting?* He can be taken to prison just for being at a meeting. He can be kept there for a year without even being charged for anything. *What if he is beaten and tortured?* That happens to lots of boys.

The teacher moves on to geography, but I don't. *And what of Tariq? How could Tariq survive prison?* I remember my mother's words: *Tariq has a place where words don't live. It is deep inside of him.* I wonder, *Would he go into that place and stay there forever?*

When I come out of school, I look around for Hamid, but I do not see him. *Where is he?*

Rula and I wait awhile, but he still doesn't show up.

I begin to wonder if something is wrong. "Maybe something happened to Hamid," I finally say to her. "I am so worried about him. I wish I could talk to you about my fears for him, but I can't. It's not safe. I think I better go home."

"I will see you tomorrow, then," Rula says.

I look for Hamid all the rest of the way home. I can't find him. I go to Tariq's house, but his mother hasn't seen either Hamid or Tariq. *Where are they?*

Fear kinks my stomach. It is stronger than sadness. It tries to come up my throat, but I won't let it. I run fast, pushing it down. I head straight home on the main road and go up to the roof. I search through the streets, but I can't see Hamid. I do see Hend. She is hurrying, almost running. As she gets closer, I see that she is afraid.

"Malaak!" she calls. I hurry downstairs.

"Here I am, Hend."

"Malaak, have you seen Hamid?"

"No, I've been looking for him."

"Ay, then it must be true. I think I saw him in a car."

"What? With who?" Sweat runs down one temple. My dream flashes in my head. *Hamid in the bus.*

"Mother wouldn't like it. I've heard rumors about the young man he was with." She lowers her voice and whispers, "Religious zealot." She raises her voice. "Hamid should not be seen with him. Hurry! They are on the other side of the market."

I'm afraid Hamid will help the young man bomb something. I won't tell Hend this. I can hardly think the words myself.

"I'll come with you, Hend. Then when we get there, let me try to get Hamid out of the car."

We zigzag through the narrow streets, darting around all the people. We cut through stone passageways, through the alleys. Ahead of us is a building covered with graffiti. I see a black car. The rear window is spider-webbed with cracks. The fender is dented in. One taillight is gone. The young man is driving. Hamid and Tariq are in the back, and the car is going slow. We run toward it. I'm faster than Hend, and I go for the front of the car. Hend tries to grab the right back-door handle but spins off. I hear a curse from inside the car, and it begins to slow. I run in front of the car. I close my eyes and wait for the car to hit me. The brakes squeal, Hend screams, and Hamid is shouting.

Then I'm falling. When I open my eyes, Tariq is staring into my eyes. The brown in his eyes has gold flecks in it. Behind the brown is a flickering. *What is that flickering?* Hend and Hamid are standing behind Tariq.

"You must have a lump on your head, but there is no blood," Tariq says. When I don't answer, he goes on. "No one hit you. You fainted."

I try to raise my head, but it makes me dizzy. I close my eyes. "You are very brave, Malaak," Tariq says.

"I don't think so," I say. "Brave is my father." I open my eyes and smile at him, but the smile feels lopsided.

Hamid starts yelling at Hend. "What are you doing here? Malaak could have been killed."

Hend shouts back, "Why are you here? Why are you with him?" She points to the young man from the meeting. "I've heard about him."

Hamid keeps yelling as if he hadn't heard Hend. "Get out of here. I won't let you stop me, Hend."

"Stop you? Stop you from what?" Hend screams. Her arms and back are straight, rigid, but she bunches her hands into fists.

I stand up. My hand burns, and I see I've scraped it again. Then my knee throbs, both knees. I'm full of scrapes. Tears hover in my eyes and finally spill over. Tariq stands beside me. We both look at Hend and Hamid.

Hamid's hands punch the air with each word. Each punch gets closer to Hend. "Get out of here. Get out of here."

"We're not leaving without you," Hend says.

My voice shakes as I say to Hamid, "If you don't come now, I will not keep the promise I made when you gave me the flag." He turns to face me. His mouth opens and closes. His arms drop to his sides, but his left hand still curls and uncurls.

Hamid looks at the young man from the rally. I'd forgotten him. "See you later, Khalid," Hamid says, then turns and starts walking.

Hend, Tariq, and I follow him. I can't help but sneak some looks at Tariq as we walk. I wonder if he will say more.

He walks at my side, and finally he says, "Malaak, did you know that I was with my father when he died? I was bending over him, just like I bent over you, only there was blood everywhere. He was shot several times. I could see the bone in his shoulder. There were pieces of his muscle showing. I tried to put all the pieces back in, but it didn't help. He died anyway. When I looked at you today, I remembered that moment, but this time I knew it wouldn't be my fault if you didn't live. It wasn't my fault then either. No one can put all the pieces back together."

I sense Tariq waiting, so I nod.

"You love Hamid, so you do what you can. I loved my father, but . . ." His voice faded. After a few minutes he said, "I'm glad you're all right, Malaak."

"Well, not quite all right. I know I will be sore all over tomorrow."

Tariq just laughs, and I know that something is different in him. The wounded dog didn't laugh.

SOLDIERS

❧

I can't sleep. It must be very late. The smell of cinnamon drifts in my room. I wonder if Mother is making *sahlab*. When I go to the kitchen, Hend and Mother are sipping cups of it. "Would you like some *sahlab*?" Mother asks. "Join us for a treat." She ladles the steamy milk into a tin cup and hands it to me.

There is a pounding on the front door. The sound is much harder than fists. Hend drops her cup. Her face pales. Then red spots burn in her cheeks. Hamid comes running down the stairs.

"Why are the soldiers here at this time of night?" Mother walks slowly to the door. The pounding comes again.

"Run to the roof, Hamid! Hide!" Hend whispers.

"Open up," a soldier shouts. Have they come to get Hamid?

Mother opens the door, with Hend right behind her. Two Israeli soldiers are standing there. One is tall, with fierce eyebrows and a gray-streaked beard. The other is short, with a pudgy face and a belly that hangs over his belt. He looks young.

"You need to pay your electric bill," the short soldier says. My mother's mouth drops. A small squeak escapes from it. Hend giggles.

"Wha-whaaat?" Mother finally stutters. I know if I look at Hend, I'm in trouble. I try to keep my face tight. Mother turns her back on the soldiers and frowns at us.

"Your electric bill," the other, bigger soldier says. "It's late."

"Oh," Mother says. "Yes, it is nearly midnight."

"No," the pudgy soldier says. "Your bill is late." A laugh finally bursts out. I can't stop it. Two minutes ago, I thought they were going to arrest my brother, and instead, they are asking for a late bill. Added to that is the fact that my mother can't figure out if the bill is late or the hour. Pretty soon Hend and I are bent over, hugging our ribs. Tears run down our faces. My stomach muscles hurt.

I think Mother is trying to figure out who is crazier — the soldiers or Hend and I. She goes back to the kitchen and comes out with money in her hand.

"Here." She pushes the money into the taller soldier's hand. They leave. Mother shuts the door and turns around to look at us.

"Lorette told me they were doing this last week, but I forgot. Are you girls crazy? You could have been shot." Lorette is my mother's friend, who lives close by. She is a Palestinian Christian. Mother shrugs and looks around the room. "Where is Hamid?" I am too weak to talk.

"Upstairs," Hend says.

"Get him," my mother says, and I stop laughing. Her mouth is tight. I see that the vein in her temple is jumping. She leans against the wall, waiting. I sit at the long table at the end of the room.

It is not far to the roof, but it seems a long time before Hend and Hamid come into the sitting room. Hend is looking at Mother, but Hamid is staring at me. I shake my head slightly from side to side.

"Why did you tell him to hide, Hend? Did you think the soldiers were looking for him?" Mother asks.

"You fool," Hamid says to Hend.

"You are the fool, Hamid." Hend's voice is high. "Tell her. You tell her. If you don't, I will."

"I am too young for Islamic Jihad now, but I will join. Meanwhile I will help fight in any way I can."

My mother jerks backward and then bends over at the waist. She gags as if she is trying not to vomit. Her hands fly to her mouth. She straightens. Words jag out from between her hands. "How . . . could . . . you . . . be . . . part . . . of a group that killed your father? How could you bomb someone?"

Mother takes her hands from her mouth and holds them in front of her as if she is begging. She says, "No son . . ." and then begins to cry. Tears splash on her upturned palms. She tries again and gets out, "No son of mine will ever be a member of Islamic Jihad." Then she cries harder.

"I—" Hamid says, and then stops because she is turning away from him. She flings out her hands like a blind woman feeling in front of her in order to see. Her hand hits the gilded Jerusalem picture on the wall, and it falls to the floor. The glass shatters and the frame splits.

Mother continues walking with her hands out as if feeling the wall, but she is walking across the room to the stairs to the second floor. Didn't she hear the picture fall?

Hend looks at Hamid and screams, "You must stay away from Islamic Jihad! Do you hear?" Then she runs after Mother.

I pick up the picture and try to pull the photograph from the broken frame, but I see that blood is dripping from my hand. I do not even feel pain because the broken glass inside me is ripping at my guts, my throat.

I fear the glass will rip out of me, so I jerk at the broken frame. Stupid frame makes me angry anyway. It can't be repaired. I rip the top piece off and throw it into the corner.

The pain in my left hand throbs badly now. When I had jerked the frame off, I'd held on even more tightly with that hand, and the cut is even deeper. I must get the photograph out before I bleed on it and mess it up. I pull at the photograph and it comes out, but a corner is ripped off.

And then the pain rips out of me, and I can't stop it. I sit down on the floor. I gulp the air in great rushing breaths. The tears come down my cheeks as I press on my hand to stop the bleeding. "I've ripped it," I say.

I go to the kitchen to get a rag to wrap my hand. Then I return and pick up the photograph and take the other picture of our family off the wall too.

All this time Hamid has been staring at the space where Mother was when he first said the words *I will join.* I walk over to him. Right now Mother has Hend. Hamid needs me. I look into his eyes. They are deep. Far down inside them are my mother's words: *No son of mine will ever be a member of Islamic Jihad.* I take Hamid's hand, and we walk to the roof. He looks at the moon.

I look at the photographs until I grow sleepy. I stand up to go downstairs, and Hamid stands too.

"Don't be upset, Malaak. You only ripped the picture. Mother's life was already ripped." I look at Mother's picture through my tears. Hamid says, "It will never be Jerusalem 1946 again, and it will never be our family again. Father, Mother, Hend, you, and me. That picture is ripped too."

We go down the roof stairs and into the house. Hamid follows me into my bedroom and says in a voice that echoes in the still house, "I will not join Islamic Jihad. I will not bomb." And then it is quiet.

TRUCE

∽

In the morning, I get up with Mother and Hend. When they pray, I add my own special thanks on the end. "And thank you, God, that Hamid will not join Islamic Jihad, or help the boy who was driving the car."

All day long I feel so happy about Hamid. On the way home from school, Rula and I decide that I will go to her house tomorrow if it is all right with my mother. After Rula turns down her street, Hamid and I pass a group of women who follow the beliefs of a strict Islamic group. Their black veils fall from their heads to their feet. They cluster together and stare with their slivered, crow eyes. I shudder and cross the street.

Hamid has speeded up his walking. I pick up my pace, but the skin on my forearms prickles and the little hairs stand up. I'm being watched. It isn't the black-veiled women. They are behind me now and talking among themselves. I stop and look across our narrow street. There is an Israeli soldier standing not far from our house. This is new. The soldier doesn't look much older than Hend. He sways back and forth, from right foot to left foot. His face is bony. His left hand pulls at the corner of a narrow mustache. He scans the street. I look down before his eyes reach me, but I can feel them follow me home.

Why is he there? To watch for violence?

I thought that Hamid had come into the house, but he isn't here. He must have gone into the alley. I go through to the alley but don't see him.

I hurry up to the roof to feed Abdo, and while I'm up there, I look for Hamid. That soldier frightens me. I remember Hamid's words: *What is safe . . . anymore?* He must be out with Tariq. I strain forward, watching. Then I see Hamid come out of Tariq's house.

The soldier is staring down the street to where Hamid and Tariq are. I edge closer. I feel strings inside of me, stretching. The soldier watches Hamid cross to our side of the street. He watches Hamid enter our house. I step back and bend to pick up Abdo. I hear *clomp, clomp, clomp, clomp.* Hamid and Tariq come out onto the roof. Hamid ducks down and crawls to where I am with Abdo.

"Is the soldier still there?" he asks.

"Yes."

He crawls back across the roof, drops something, and goes down with Tariq.

I walk to the stairs and see that Hamid has placed a stone by the stairs. There is another one too. Maybe Tariq put it there.

They must be planning to throw stones from the roof. Usually boys throw stones in the street. I pick up the stones, but my arms feel so heavy with the weight of them that I want to put them back right away. They are pulling me down, sinking me.

Even though Hamid will not join Islamic Jihad, he is still a fighter. A stone fighter with a rock fist. He will not give up, so I carry the stones downstairs and sneak into the back alley and drop them there, under the clothesline.

That night, at the evening meal, the air is tight. Hamid's eyes are broody, and his eyebrows are drawn together when he looks up at me. He looks back down, tears his bread apart, and doesn't talk. There is a quiet between Mother and Hamid. And there is a quiet that comes to sit in my stomach. I don't like it. It takes up space, and I was already having a hard time eating. So I just give up.

This quiet is not like before. It is not the squeeze of the dark, or a wordless space pulling me in. I know what this quiet is. It is the stretched-out quiet of last night, a quiet of unsaid words, ripped pieces, and shattered glass. All the things that can't be fixed. I look at Hamid's bowed head.

As I lie in bed, I hear soft shuffles overhead. Someone is on the roof. It must be Hamid. And then I realize what else was in my stomach at supper, why I couldn't eat in the first place. It was a fist. A cold fist of fear.

Watch him, Abdo. I wing my thought through the ceiling and up to the roof. After a while it is quiet again. I think about going to Rula's house tomorrow. When I asked Mother in the afternoon, she said that it was all right. Thoughts of going to Rula's house don't worry me, so I fall asleep.

THE INCIDENT

In the morning, I run to the roof to feed Abdo, and then I look to see if stones are there. I see some, so I carry them downstairs and hide them under my mattress. I'll take them outside later, when no one is watching.

After school, on the way to Rula's house, the street is quiet. Hamid doesn't speak as he walks us to Rula's. There is a warning in the quiet. A woman in a turquoise dress looks at me from her arched stone doorway, her hand tight on her child's arm. She doesn't smile. Her face is creased with worry lines. She is murmuring, "God is greater, God is greater."

Rula lives in a downstairs apartment in a square block building. We enter the sunshiny warmth of the living room, where Rula's mother is sitting on the sofa. Her face is thin. She has dark rings under her eyes. She is wearing a blue-and-rose striped *thaub,* and a white gauzy *hijab.* "Welcome."

"This is my mother, Fida," Rula says, "and this"—she gestures to another woman who stands in the doorway—"is my aunt Halima."

"Peace be upon you," Halima says.

"And upon you," I reply.

Rula's mother holds out her arms to Rula, and Rula runs over and sits beside her on the sofa. They hug each other.

Halima brings tea and cakes. I sink into this world of food and light. The three of them are talking, but I'm not even listening. I am settled into the safe space, surrounded by the warm hum of voices.

We talk for a while. Then Rula kisses her mother on the cheek, and we go to the bedroom. Beside the bed Rula has a tablet of paper. I grab the tablet and begin to draw birds. Then half of the picture becomes an olive grove, and the birds are flying over it. The other half becomes a two-story house with many windows and balconies.

"Malaak," Rula says, "you are very good. You can be an artist when you grow up. Your pictures will make you famous. They will be put in museums in Jerusalem. And then, of course, we'll have to go see them."

I laugh and tell her I haven't done enough drawing. "I am going to be a poet. Hamid used to write poetry, Rula. He has a whole notebook of poems. But he says there isn't time for things like that now."

Rula lowers her chin and says in a deep voice, "There are more important things for us to do these days." She sounds just like Hamid.

"You must not let him know that I told you about his poem writing. He doesn't think he is very good at it. But I think his poems are special."

"It's okay, Malaak. I won't say anything."

"Do you remember when we were waiting for him after school and I was very worried because he didn't show up? It was because he wanted to join Islamic Jihad someday. He went to religious meetings. I was so afraid, but now he won't join. That is why I can even say something to you."

"I understand why you were so afraid."

"But I'm still afraid."

"Why?"

"He is putting stones on the roof to throw at someone. I carried them downstairs, but I don't think that will stop him. I don't want him to be in any fighting at all. I lost my father, and I do not want to lose him."

"I can understand that. My father is in prison, and my mother was so sick, I was afraid she would die. I couldn't have stood it."

Halima calls from the other room. "Come, Rula. Come, Malaak. We will walk to Malaak's home."

As we leave her room, Rula squeezes my hand and whispers, "I won't tell anyone about Hamid."

The three of us walk toward my house. When I am at my street corner, I thank them, and they turn around to go home.

The soldier is still across the street, only his legs are stiff, not swaying. As I get closer, I can see that there is a thick rope of muscle in his jaw and neck. His hand does not pull at his mustache. It holds his gun across the front of his body like a shield. His eyes train on each person, each movement. Something must have happened. He stares at me, and then I know. He is afraid. He is all alone here on my street, and he is scared like me.

"Has something happened?" I cry, bursting into the house. *Did Hamid do something?* is what I mean. I hear sounds in the kitchen, and I run there. Hend is cooking.

"Is Hamid home?" I ask.

"No. He was here earlier today, with Tariq."

I run up to the roof. In the corner are more stones. Hamid is still fighting with stones. I look over the edge of the roof at the soldier. He is looking up at me. I duck, catching quick breaths, but the blood pounds in my ears, my face, my eyes. I close my eyes.

Then I open them, and Abdo is sitting on my knee, looking at me. I stay on the roof awhile.

When it is time for the evening meal, I go downstairs to eat. I'm greeted by Hamid's shouts.

Tariq is close on his heels. The relief I feel at seeing them is gone with Hamid's words.

"An incident," he says.

"What kind of incident?" Hend asks.

"Sit down and eat with us," my mother says to Tariq.

"And then you can tell us," Hend says.

I feel the clenched hand in my stomach, the fullness that won't let me eat. But I am determined to eat. I grab a piece of cheese. I eat falafel and tomato sauce. *Hamid is safe,* I say to myself. *Incidents do not matter.*

"An Israeli was driving to his home in the Gush Katif settlement, near the Khan Yunis refugee camp. His car broke down, and he went to get help. His yellow license plate was spotted," Hamid says.

Tariq picks up the story. "A man shot him."

Mother brings in some oranges. "Here, have some water," I say to Tariq. I drink a whole glass of water myself. I think I have room for an orange.

"Will there be a curfew?" Hend asks.

"I imagine," Tariq answers.

My mother moans. "Killing settlers. It's not right. It will bring more trouble."

"They are bringing in more soldiers. Setting up outposts in the city," Hamid says.

Hot tea soaks down my throat. I pick up an orange, then put it back down on the table. All that eating did not push the fear out. It is still there.

Tariq grabs an orange, turns to my mother, and thanks her for the meal. Then he leaves. Hend, Hamid, and I sit and watch TV, but I'm not sure what the program is. I'm just staring.

EXPLOSIONS

∾

My mother calls me for breakfast. I stumble out of bed, eat, and go back upstairs to lie down for just a moment. I wake up later, and it seems very bright. Why didn't Mother wake me for school? I go into the kitchen and find her flattening some dough. "Why didn't you call me for school?"

"After the incident last night, the authorities closed the schools again."

The story comes back to me. I peek out the door. The street is deserted. I glance to the corner to see if the soldier is still there, but he is not.

Then we hear a sound like ten cracks of lightning at one time. An explosion! After a minute or two, I feel a shuddering that shakes our house, and then I hear the rumble of stones and blocks crumbling and falling. I look at my mother. She is crying.

"They are blowing up homes," she whispers. "Retaliation for the incident."

Hamid comes down the stairs and into the room, and we hear another explosion—louder than the first? "It sounds close. I wonder if it is in Beach Camp. It sounds like more than one house," he says.

I huddle next to Hend, covering my ears with my hands. She does the same. Beach Camp is only about a fifteen-minute walk from Rimal. Then there is another explosion. *Make them stop.* These words remind me of how I'd asked my father to make the rain stop, when I was little. The rain didn't stop then, and there is one more explosion now.

"People will be too angry after this." My mother has stopped crying. She shakes her head and goes into the kitchen.

When the noise ends, I hurry to the roof to see if Abdo is okay. There is dust in the air and I sweep my arms through it as soon as I step out, but this only stirs it up more. I cover my mouth and nose with my hand and breathe slowly.

But Abdo isn't there. The explosions were close. They were the loudest noises ever to come near our house. Did they scare Abdo away? I wait up on the roof all afternoon, but he doesn't come back. I hear the call for afternoon prayer. I go downstairs for supper. We are quiet during supper.

After we eat, I go back to the roof. Hamid comes and sits beside me.

"I'm afraid that Abdo is gone for good. The explosions were too close, and I think he got scared," I say.

"Could be, Malaak."

"Father sent him to me."

"I know. He knew that you needed him."

"Yes," I say.

"Maybe Father also knows that Abdo needs to fly — fly far away because that's what birds need." Then Hamid says his "Little Bird" poem.

> *"Little bird, little bird,*
> *why don't you fly?*

Are the fences too high?
Are the boundaries too big?
Are you lost or hungry?
Are you lonely or sick?
Let me see your wings.
Little bird, they are clipped.

Little bird, little bird,
don't look at the sky.
Just sing in the dust.
Just scratch in the sand.
Just hop in holes.
Just peck till you bleed.
The stones are your food,
and your nest is the street."

"You're probably right, Hamid. I do want Abdo to fly away to a safe place. But I'll miss him." My eyes get wet.

"And you will still come up here to look for him. Come, let's go downstairs." He pulls me up.

In the morning, there is still no school. Mother and Hend go to work. Hamid leaves the house, and I go with him. He doesn't stop me. We walk in silence. Hamid keeps looking down the alleys. There are so few people on the streets. We are winding our way toward the sea, where Beach Camp is.

I'm glad I'm with him; he will have to protect me. Maybe it will keep him from doing something dangerous.

We are at the edge of the camp where the bombing was. A huge crowd is gathered there.

A twisted piece of concrete with steel rods sticking out at crazy angles tells me where a house was. Beside the concrete is a pile of blackened cloth and wood. A chair? Sunlight glitters off pieces of glass scattered among the chunks of wall. A young woman scuffs through this skeleton house. Her face is smudged with soot. Her dark eyes pick among the ashes, looking for something.

A man tells Hamid, "The Israelis bombed the house of a man whose nephew was suspected of being an instigator."

"An instigator of what?" I ask Hamid.

The man hears me and says, "No one knows

what the nephew was accused of. He'd never been tried for anything. Look at the woman poking among the ruins. I heard that she and her husband had just moved up to their own floor of the family house. A new floor. They waited for five years to get a building permit."

But five other houses on the block had been bombed too. As examples. Murmurs rise from all over the crowd. They swell into an anger that runs through it, punching men and boys.

"Hey!" a man yells at me. I'd been backing up without realizing it, and I'd stepped on his foot. I jump and bump into Hamid.

"Malaak, come." Hamid pulls my hand. "We've got to get out of here before something happens."

As we walk away, he says, "That poor young woman. That could be Hend. She's waiting for the intifada to be over, she's waiting for money, she's waiting for marriage, she's waiting for a building permit. She's waiting for her building to be bombed."

"Wait-and-see Hend," I say. What Hamid said is true. Poor Hend. The thought of her waiting life is sad. I sigh and her burdens leave me. We walk home.

The next day only the primary schools are open. Hamid walks me to school. He speaks to his friends along the way. As he leaves me at school, I see the flare in his eyes. A warning? What will he do?

At school, I whisper to Rula about the bombing.

"My mother would never let me go see that," she says.

"Neither would mine," I tell her. "She and Hend were working, and I went with Hamid."

"You are so brave, Malaak."

We are reading about trees. I read one line about eucalyptus trees and close my eyes to see the silvery leaves, but instead I picture burned branches of furniture with shreds of clothing hanging from them.

I read another line, about palm trees with sturdy trunks. I see a tree, its leaves circling up to the sun like upturned hands. But the tree becomes a fragile young woman poking down, down into the blackened leftovers.

I wish I hadn't seen the houses.

STONES

∾

After school, Rula goes home with her aunt. Hamid is waiting for me, but he salutes, laughs, and runs. He is bounding from person to person along the street. He is full of energy. *Nerves,* Hend would say. I rush to keep up with him, but he is jagging back and forth across the street.

"Hamid, Hamid, wait. Slow down."

He looks back at me and laughs. "Sorry," he says. He stops at the tomato vendor we pass every day after school and pulls the cigarette from the man's hand. He puffs on it, coughs, throws it on the ground, and runs across the street. He reaches the two old card players, steals a card from their game, smacks it into the middle of his forehead, kisses it, and throws it over his shoulder.

I've never seen Hamid so stirred up. I want to catch him and tie him up. What will he do next? We reach the corner of our street and turn down it.

Hamid takes off running toward our house. Tariq runs from his house after Hamid. He must have been looking for him. Were they up on the roof, waiting for a soldier to come, before Hamid came to get me? Is he jumpy and stirred up because he thinks he will have a stone battle? A jeep roars up behind me.

I spring back, slamming into someone's wall. It almost knocks the breath out of me. In the jeep is the soldier from our street. He climbs out of the jeep and goes into a building across the street from our house. My arms are out on each side of me. I'm pushing on the wall. I want to slow this down. It's all moving much too fast. Then I'm walking toward our house. Hamid and Tariq turn into the little space beside it.

I hear stomping and look up. The soldier is standing on the roof across the street, putting on a helmet. That building must be an outpost. Israeli soldiers set up lookout places in different buildings in the city when they think there is going to be violence. I step into the street and look up at our roof.

Hamid's face peers from the roof along with Tariq's. They took the back stairs up there. A giant hand inside me throws me toward our house. I'm screaming, "No, no, no!"

I pump my legs and hands as hard as I can. I go through the house and run up the roof stairs. When I'm almost there, the soldier yells. "Drop the stones. Stop throwing." His voice shakes. He is so afraid. *Oh, God,* I think, *the soldier could do anything. He could shoot. Slow it all down.*

I see Hamid's upper body and his arm pulling backward. As he throws, I scream, "Stop it!" Tariq throws at the same time.

I leap the final step and run toward Hamid. He turns toward me and screams, "Get down!"

I hear the crack of the gun, and Hamid is falling on me. We fall to the roof. I bang my head and groan. Hamid is heavy on my legs.

"Hamid," I say, but he doesn't answer. "Hamid," I say again. *No, it can't be,* I think. I feel like I'm floating above us, watching, and then I hear *Do something* in my brain, and I sit up. Hamid's face is toward me, but his eyes are closed. Alarm throbs in my temples as I see the blood behind his head.

Do something.

"Help me!" I scream to Tariq, who is standing motionless, his eyes fixed on Hamid, his mouth open. He lifts Hamid's legs off mine.

"Get Mother!" I scream, and Tariq runs down the stairs. As I wait, I breathe in Hamid's blood, his sweat. I open my mouth and pant. The throbbing alarm in my temples is louder. It's filling my head. Soon there is a red pool under Hamid's head. Mother runs over with Hend right behind her. Together they pick up Hamid and carry him.

Do something.

The throbbing pounds in my ears. I run down the stairs, and Mother and Hend follow me, carrying Hamid.

I run into the street yelling, "Help us! Help us!" I see the soldier from the outpost running toward me. I scream, but he runs past me and after Tariq, who is running in and out of knots of people. Mother and Hend are trying to get through the door, with Hamid between them.

In the street Hend shouts, "We need a car!"

People come running from other houses. Soon we are in the middle of a crowd. A tall man with a broad forehead and bushy eyebrows steps from the crowd. He has thick shoulders and burly arms. "Here, let me take him." I hear the roar of jeeps coming up the street.

"Tell Tariq's mother," Mother shouts to Hend. Hend elbows through the crowd and runs toward Tariq's house.

The man with Hamid in his arms begins running, and Mother and I follow him. A car stops and we crowd in. We drive toward Ahli Arab Hospital in Palestine Square. It is the closest to us.

THE HOSPITAL

∾

We all get out of the taxi, and the man with
Hamid in his arms rushes into the hospital com-
pound. We follow him, and I blink at the sweet-
scented brightness as we go by the outer buildings,
passing flowers and bushes — daisies, bougainvillea, nasturtiums, and hibiscus. I see each bloom,
alone and clear.

We go into a small cramped emergency room.
So clean. It is bright here too. I close my eyes.
The brightness makes the throbbing in my head
worse. Maybe soldiers are pounding around inside
it with their thick boots.

A doctor comes over and examines Hamid. "It
doesn't look good. It's a head wound, and he's lost

a lot of blood. We will have to operate. Is that all right?" he asks Mother.

"Do whatever you can for him," my mother says. They take him to an operating room.

She paces in a tiny area of the emergency room. Others pull back to give her space. I sink down to the floor. I see there is blood on my shirt, my skirt. I close my eyes, but then I see Hamid's face. *What will happen to Hamid? Will he live?*

If only I had known what that restless energy meant! He and Tariq were probably up on the roof half the day planning their stone battle, waiting for a soldier to come. And yet Hamid had come to get me at school. My protector.

I see him running down the street, talking to the tomato vendor and the old men playing cards. *Oh, Hamid!*

If only I'd gotten to the roof sooner! The last time I was on the roof with Hamid, he'd helped me to see that Mother's life was already ripped and that I could not change it. *Who will help me to see now?*

The door opens and Hend comes in. Mother rushes to her, hugging her. She opens her mouth and a high-pitched whining comes out. Hend holds her for a while, stroking her back until she calms. "I found Tariq's mother and I told her what happened," says Hend. "What of Hamid?"

"We do not know much. They will operate. He was shot in the head, and they are not hopeful," Mother says. Hend covers her face with her hands and sits down. The wail of mourning comes from behind her hands.

"Shh, shh," my mother croons again and again. It sounds like a song, a lullaby. Comforting Hend now, she is kneeling in front of her, hugging her, and then she sits on the floor as Hend weeps. I pull Mother off the floor and bring a chair for her, next to Hend. I sit on the floor, beside Mother. She is moaning in a low tone. Hend is up, pacing, pacing. Now she bites her hand.

I know it will be a while until we hear anything about Hamid, so I go outside. I see a hibiscus bush, and I remember Hamid giving Rula and me the hibiscus flowers. I smell the orange blossoms, and I think of the stolen oranges that night on the way to the camp. Each thing brings back more memories of Hamid.

I was so afraid something would happen, and it did. Was there more I could have done? Maybe Hamid was right. Nothing is safe anymore. But to throw stones at soldiers on your own street is a good way to make sure of that. A stab of anger jolts me. Then I gasp. How can I be angry at Hamid when he may be dying? What will I do if he dies like Father did?

I can't stop the tears at this point, so I just sit down and cry. I feel the thought beginning to spiral inside. *He dies too, he dies too, he dies too.* I can't stop it. It is taking me down to my wordless place. I know that time is passing, but I've no idea how much. I feel like I'm caught in the dark.

I stumble back into the glare of the emergency room. I try to listen to the people talking, but my mind floats above it. Nothing makes sense. I sit down. Then I am nodding. My head hits my knees, and I give up and lie down. When I wake up, I look at my mother's face. The sagging pouches under her eyes and the lines running down from her mouth tell me we've been here for hours. It is late. The room is packed with people who must have come in while I was sleeping.

I sit up and my mother says, "We think the doctor will be here soon." I stand and then bend over to help my mother up. Hend stands up on the other side of her. The door opens and a doctor walks in, followed by a nurse.

"He survived the operation," the doctor says. A long *whoosh* of breath rushes from my mother's mouth. "But it doesn't look good," the doctor goes on. "If he does live, I'm afraid there could be permanent damage."

My mother's face is gray. No, her clothes are gray. No, it is Hend who is gray. Then I see that all the people are colorless and soundless.

The walls of the room are leaning in. The ceiling is coming down. The doctor's face is flattened, and his mouth is a line.

It is light. So light. It is quiet. The floor is coming up to join the ceiling.

THE PIECES

∽

"She fainted," a voice says. Or are there two voices and two separate words? Nothing is going together. I hear people, but I don't understand.

I try to say something, but it comes out like "Gawwww." It sounds strange. I try again, but it is only the same thing, "Gawwww." It sounds like a piece of a word, maybe just letters.

"She had a shock and she fainted." Is it the doctor? Is it his voice? Hands are on my wrist, my face.

"Oh no. No." Another voice. Is it a woman's? "Not again, please, God."

I open my eyes to a blurry brightness. I close them again. I hear crying. I'm sure it's crying. *What is happening?*

"Take her home. She just needs rest."

"But when this happened before, it took her a long time to talk. Oh, God, help us. Help us." I turn my head toward the words. *Is it Mother? It must be.*

It's as if I'm back, back there in the place of the raggedy pages. The torn newspaper in my brain. Such a clutter.

Another voice. "What if it is too much this time? First Father, then Hamid? What if she doesn't come back?" Is that Hend?

"Stop!" someone yells. I think it is my mother. "Don't even say those words."

I lift my hand and feel someone take it. I sit up and feel arms settle me as I sit. I am on a table. When I open my eyes, I see Mother and Hend. Their faces are so close to me. Peering at me. I get off the table. My legs don't feel too steady. Mother places an arm around my shoulder.

"Just get her home to a familiar place. You all need rest. There is nothing more you can do here," a nurse tells Mother.

Mother is crying. "Hush, Mother," Hend says. "She is right. You are exhausted. Let's go home."

We head out into the dark. "Stay together and close to the buildings as we walk," Hend tells us.

We huddle together toward home, and then as we turn down our road, Hend says, "Look, it is the tip of dawn." But I walk into the house, into my bedroom, and lie down on the mattress.

I close my eyes and see swirling pictures. No, just pieces. A pink hibiscus, an orange, a brown-and-white goat, a stone.

I hear laughter, shots, pounding feet, cracks of lightning. No, it is explosions.

I shiver, then sweat. And then I feel drowsiness, and I'm flying.

Bird wings carry me. *Oh, Abdo, you've come back for me.* But we are flying in mist. White mist. I'm choking. The tear gas. I gasp, breathing deeply.

I'm awake. I toss my head from side to side. Fling the pictures away.

But they gather again. Pulling me down, farther down. Red graffiti, crushed white flowers, wispy yellow grass, smoky mirages. And then I picture Father. His upraised hand, his dripping hands.

Father? Are you there? Brave Father, brave

Father. The words circle around and around. I'm slipping again, but this time it is into sleep.

Bam, bam, bam. The sound of someone banging on the front door wakes me. I go into the living room and sit on the sofa. A burly man is at the door.

"Peace be upon you," the man says.

"And upon you," Hend replies.

"How is the boy?" the man asks.

"He survived the operation, God be praised," Hend replies, and she darts a quick glance in my direction.

"I wanted you to know that the other boy has slipped away for now," he says. "Men are moving him from one hiding place to another. I want to speak to his mother, but I only knew where you lived." My mother hasn't said a word.

The other boy? Is the man talking about Tariq? Is Tariq hiding in the darkness? Or is the darkness hiding him? So much darkness. Squeezing him, squeezing me.

"His name is Tariq Ajrami. His mother, a widow, lives down the street. People can tell you where she lives," Hend says.

I look at this man. *Who is he?* I think I should know.

Hend steps forward. "You have done so much for us. We thank you for getting Hamid to the hospital. Thank you." She pauses. "I'm afraid I don't even know your name."

"I am Jamil Jamiyaa."

"And I am Hend Abed Atieh." The man turns to leave. "Thank you again. May God make you safe," Hend says. She closes the door behind him.

Mother shuffles to a chair. Hend looks at me and says, "Mother has been to the hospital already. She has seen Hamid. It is late afternoon, Malaak. Do you understand me?" I nod.

She sits down beside me. No one says anything for a minute or two. Hend kneels in front of Mother, takes Mother's face in her hands, and looks into her eyes. Then she sighs, gets up, and turns on the television. "You must get your mind out of the hospital. Put it in another place. Watch my soap opera." She goes into the kitchen. I hear her clatter around. Mother and I watch the television.

We sit at the tiny table in the kitchen. I see

hummus and pita bread. My stomach is full already. *Or is it that I can't feel in my belly? Or feel my belly?* I place my hand on my stomach. Such thoughts. What a jumble.

I leave the table and go up to my room. I sit on the mattress. I pull out Hamid's notebook of poems and read the first line of the poem he recited to me on the roof, *Little bird, little bird, why don't you fly?* I close the book. I can't read more. I close my eyes and remember Abdo. I will go to the roof. But when I am in the hallway, I hear the door downstairs open and close.

Then I hear Hend say, "What are you doing here? They could be looking for you here."

And then I hear Mother's voice. "Tariq."

"I have to see Malaak," Tariq says. "Jamil Jamiyaa told me that she fainted at the hospital and couldn't speak when she came out. Then he said that when he was here today, Malaak did not speak at all. Only sat and stared."

I begin walking down the stairs. "Hend, I am afraid for her," he says. I come into the living room. "Malaak, you were so brave," Tariq says.

"You tried to save Hamid. I saw you. I know how you love Hamid. Do not go into that quiet place. Please. Hamid needs you now."

Looking into Tariq's eyes, I see that he knows. He knows what I feel. He knows the confusion, the swirling thoughts. He knows how hard it is.

"Here," Tariq says. He hands me his little *taqiya*. "Take this to Hamid for me. Please, Malaak. I know I can trust you."

Hend comes over and grabs him by the shoulder. "Quick, you must leave." Tariq opens the door and slips into the darkness outside.

Mother comes over and puts her arms around me. "My brave Malaak." I sit down on the sofa. Mother leaves. When she comes back, she has a little blanket. "Sleep here. I will leave the light in the kitchen on." Hend goes up to Mother's room, and I hear her radio. The music is soft. My mother bends over and kisses me on the forehead. "May you reach morning in goodness. My brave Malaak. You are so much like your father."

I close my eyes. The pictures swirl, Hamid's white face and the flutter of a bird wing, but I still hear my mother's words: *My brave Malaak. You are so much like your father.* I still see the look in Tariq's eyes. *Hamid needs me.* Tariq is right. I say Mother's bravery words in my mind. *Bravery is not seen in one act. It is measured by the choices in the night,* over and over until I can't anymore.

When I wake, I see that my mother is folding clothes on the long table. I hear Hend's radio and wonder if she left it on all night. I sit up.

"Good morning, Malaak. Actually I should say, good late morning, Malaak."

"I want to see Hamid," I say to Mother. My voice is thick. My tongue feels big in my mouth. My mother just looks at me. In my hand is Tariq's *taqiya.* I get up and go into the kitchen. I put the *taqiya* on the table and pour a glass of orange juice. I drink it down without stopping. I am so thirsty. And my stomach is growling. I realize I haven't eaten for almost two days. I get some bread and cheese.

THE RAIN

∽

While I am eating, Hend comes into the kitchen. "Mother says that you want to see Hamid. Are you sure, Malaak?"

I nod because my mouth is full. Then I pick up the *tuqiya*. I say, "I must give him this."

"But, Malaak, he does not look so good," Hend says. "I saw him yesterday before you woke up." Mother shakes her head at Hend. I think she is saying, *Enough, be quiet.* But I am not sure.

After I dress we all leave the house. As we walk along our street, so many people stop us. "Thanks be to God for your safety," they say to me. "May God bless you and Hamid," they say to my mother. We turn the corner and continue walking. The two old card-playing men stand up and wave at me. My eyes tear up. Hamid has so many friends.

As we get to the next street, Mother says, "Malaak, I want you to know that Hamid is in a coma. That means that he is not conscious. It is like he is sleeping, but he does not wake up."

"The nurse told me yesterday that he did not know that I was there. But I know Hamid. He is listening for us. He hears our voices. I am sure of it," Hend says.

"And I am sure he is waiting for your voice, Malaak," Mother says.

I want to run ahead, but I continue to walk beside Mother and Hend. We go through the outer courtyard, and I do not stop to look at the flowers. We go into the hospital through the women's ward. It is clean, and on the wall is a bronze plaque. Someone behind me begins to read in English. Then someone says in Arabic, "To the memory of Captain Ivor Jones, born at Wales, 1895. Educated at the Leys School, Cambridge. Fell at Gaza, March twenty-sixth, 1917." As I go up the stairs, I realize that those must be the English words on the plaque.

A nurse recognizes my mother and says, "I'm afraid there is no change."

I look along the row of beds, and at the end is Hamid. His head is bandaged. Bottles above his bed drip something into tubes that go into his arms. A machine blinks and makes a low humming sound above his bed.

Fell at Gaza.

I pull Tariq's *taqiya* out of my pocket and put it under Hamid's hand, which is resting on the bed. I stare at his bandaged head. It looks so round and white like the full moon. Hamid's eyes are closed. His black lashes are the smudges on the moon. He doesn't move. The blinking lights above his bed are like the stars.

Fell at Gaza. Fell at Gaza.

I look at his face to see if he hears me. But he is still. So still. So quiet. I want to say, "This is from Tariq. He wanted you to have it," but I can't. I am being squeezed. I can't look at Hamid's face anymore. I turn and run downstairs and out into the courtyard. I collapse on the ground and bury my face in my arms. Hend follows me. I feel her standing near, but she is quiet. Then I hear her feet as she walks away and comes back. I look up, and she kneels beside me. She is holding a hibiscus flower. A white one. She puts the flower in my hand.

Mother joins us, and we walk into the street. "Let's go home," Mother says. The call to prayer leads us through the huddled houses and back alleys. When we get to our house, I go up to the roof and look for Abdo, but he still isn't there. I want to look into Abdo's eyes. I want to fly away. The need to fly is so strong in me today. I felt it in the crush of darkness at the hospital. It was so hard being there with Hamid. I don't know if I can do it again, if I can see Hamid and not go flying away.

I stare at the moon. And then a white flutter separates me from the face of the moon. It settles on the corner of the roof. But it is not Abdo. It is a wild bird. It stays on the corner of the porch, watching me.

"Hello, bird." At the sound of my voice, the wild bird rises, circling up and up, catching each current until he is only a bit of shadow on the moon. Then he is gone.

Father had sent me Abdo when I needed him. "Help me again, Father," I say. I go downstairs and fall onto my mattress. I say Mother's bravery words over and over until I fall asleep.

The call to morning prayer wakes me. My heart is racing, and I am smiling. I dreamed the moon dream about my father. He went to the moon by jumping from star to star. When he was almost there, he turned and gave me the I-am-winning signal. His other hand was behind his back. I signaled to him, and then I ran the other way, circling the moon until I caught him and hugged him. I felt something in the hand behind his back. "Let me stay here with you," I said. But he didn't answer. He just kissed me. Then he brought his hand out from behind his back. In it was the flag. The Palestinian flag.

I sit up. Father came to me last night. He knows that Hamid needs me. Father wants me to stay with Hamid. "Oh, Father," I say, "you must believe that I can help Hamid."

I put on my clothes and go out of the bedroom. "Mother is making the rounds of officials, trying to get Hamid transferred to a better hospital in Israel," Hend tells me. "None of the hospitals in Gaza have the equipment or supplies that the ones in Israel do. If he needs more surgery, he should be in Israel." She hands me a bag of wet clothes. "Here, you can hang these clothes on the line."

I take them into the back alley. I remember the last time I hung up the clothes. It seems like years ago. I pin up Mother's black skirt and my two school uniforms. Then I hang up Hamid's purple T-shirt. I go back inside. Hend is in the kitchen, so I go in and watch her making bread. She seems to enjoy whacking it.

"This morning is taking so long," I tell her. I sweep each room in the house. Even the roof. When I come back downstairs, the door opens and Mother comes in. I can see that it is not good news. There is a ridge between her eyebrows, and wrinkles around her narrowed eyes. Her lips are pinched. When her words come out they are like small explosions.

"They will not move him to a hospital in Israel. In fact, they are doing what they usually do; they are moving him right now to Shifa Hospital." Hend moans. Shifa Hospital is the government hospital. No one ever wants to go there. On the back of the hospital is graffiti that says YES TO DEATH AND STARVATION.

Hamid will need me more than ever, I think. I close my eyes and picture Father's flag. *I will take the flag to Hamid today.* But then I remember that there will be soldiers posted on top of Shifa Hospital. I will have to get the flag past them. The muscles in my legs and arms tense with the thought.

"Come, Mother. You must eat, and then we will go there this afternoon," Hend says. She is talking like she is the mother. I hate it when she does this.

After we eat, I go to my room and carefully fold the flag. I smell it one last time for the scent of Father. I put it under my shirt, put a sweater on, and wrap a bulky green scarf of Mother's around my neck. I drape it across my stomach. When Hend sees me, she says, "You can't be cold."

I just say, "I am," and walk out of the door ahead of her. We are going very fast. I think that Mother is still angry. People talk to us along the way, but Mother just nods shortly. I think her mind is on seeing Hamid. We walk down Omar al-Moktar. I look at the windows in the small offices as we walk by. Many are shuttered. Vendors crowd the streets. One is selling rattan chairs, which he keeps grabbing out of the way of cars. A car honks and just misses the man. Two men in business suits are arguing at a corner. I watch their arms rise and fall as they step back and forth. *Is everyone angry?*

I see some walls with purple bougainvillea peeking over them. Finally, we are across the street from the hospital. I look up and see the soldiers on the roof. They point down at us and laugh. I tighten my arms across my chest, look down, and rush across the street. I almost trip over a blood-stained stretcher in front of the hospital.

Mother grabs my elbow. "One step and one step," she says to me.

I gulp deep breaths of air. I feel like I might vomit. Hend screams as a wild cat runs out of the hospital. This sends the soldiers into fresh rounds of laughter. We step into the hospital. The walls are grimy. "One step and one step," I say to myself.

I break from Mother's grasp and run up the stairs. Hamid is only one bed away from the stairs. His head is still wrapped, but the sheet is under his arms. One shoulder is bare; the other is wrapped with gauze, like layers of feathers. I drop to my knees beside his bed. I pick up the sheet that is under his wrapped arm. Then I pull out the flag and slip it under the sheet.

I lean forward to whisper to Hamid, but Mother gets to the top of the stairs and says, "Malaak, are you praying?" I shake my head no. I keep kneeling by Hamid's bed, with my hand on his arm.

Mother and Hend go stand on the other side of Hamid. Hend fusses with his sheet. I want her to stop. Mother talks to Hamid about the hospital, the officials she spoke with, and all the details of our walk to the hospital. It seems she is talking just to talk.

I look for a little sign that Hamid can hear us. Even a slight blink. There is nothing. After a while, Hend says, "Mother, I think we should go. You've had a long day." They turn to leave, but I stay where I am. They begin to walk.

I lean forward and whisper, "I know you can feel the flag. It is my best piece of Father."

"Come, Malaak," Mother says.

I clear my throat. "No, Mother. I want to say goodbye to Hamid by myself."

"Okay, a minute more. We'll wait here by the stairs."

I whisper to Hamid again, "Father told me in a dream to bring it to you. He didn't leave me, and I won't leave you. I will be back to see you as much as I can, and I will bring the flag each time I come. I can't leave it here with you because someone might find it, and there are soldiers at this hospital." I lift Hamid's arm and slip the flag out and put it under my sweater.

"Malaak, come," Mother says. "Let's go." I stand up. They are going down the stairs.

The soldiers on the roof are singing. Their words are slurred. Hend says, "It sounds like they are drunk," and we run across the street. A hospital van that takes patients to their homes is there. The driver motions us to jump in.

"I don't like the looks of those soldiers," he said. "I'll take you home tonight."

"Oh, thank you," Hend says. Mother sighs.

We jolt along in the van. It seems to hit each pothole, but I don't mind. My eyes are closed, and I'm singing inside. *I did it. I did it.*

I outran the darkness.

I took the flag to Hamid.

I hug the flag tight to me. I touch both Hamid and Father when I hold the flag.

When we get home, I run to the roof. I want to yell, but it is too late. I look out, but I don't see Abdo. The sun has set. I see a huge row of pink clouds, and I hear the call to prayer. I hear Mother and Hend. They are in the kitchen. Their voices drift up to me.

I decide that I will come up here each morning to send my thoughts to Hamid. I will think, *You are a fighter. You will live. You are a fighter. You will live.* I feel the strength in these words. They will keep him going until I can see him each day.

I look up into the sky. The clouds block the moon. A drop of rain hits my face. And then another and another. I hear Father's voice: *Ah, Malaak, don't you know that in Gaza when it rains, it means that God is smiling? He knows how much we need the rain.*

I open my mouth and eat the raindrops. *Thank you, Father.*

Glossary

There is no standard method of transliteration from Arabic to English. The spellings below are those most commonly used in current books on Islamic culture.

Arafat, Yasir The recognized leader of the PLO.

atayif A dessert made of rolled-up pancakes stuffed with nuts.

hajj The annual trip to Mecca that is required of Muslims at least once in their lives. It is one of the five pillars or duties of the faith.

hijab A veil or head covering worn by Muslim women. In Gaza it is usually a white scarf.

hummus Middle Eastern dish made of chickpeas.

iftar The evening meal that is eaten to break the daylight fast during the month of Ramadan.

imam A religious leader of a Muslim community.

intifada Means "shaking off." It refers to the uprising that began in December 1987 in the Occupied Territories of the West Bank and Gaza Strip.

Islamic Jihad A militant, extremist Islamic group. It officially began to operate in the Occupied Territories in 1980.

jalabiya A long loose robe worn by Muslims. This attire is considered traditional.

jihad Means "struggle" or "effort," but it can mean the defense of faith as in an armed struggle or war.

jilbab A long tunic coat worn by Muslim women in Gaza.

keffiyeh A black-and-white or red-and-white checked men's headdress.

mahshi A dish of vegetables stuffed with rice.

Mecca A city in Saudi Arabia that has the most sacred Islamic shrines.

minaret A slender tower attached to a mosque. It is used to call the people to prayer.

mosque A center for public worship for Muslims.

muezzin The person who issues the call to prayer.

mukhtar The head or leader of a village.

PLO Palestine Liberation Organization. The secular, nationalist organization made up of many Palestinian groups that was recognized by the United Nations as the legitimate representative of the Palestinian people.

Qur'an Means "discourse" or "recitation." This book is the body of revelations given by God and received by Muhammad.

Ramadan The Muslim holy month, during which fasting from dawn to sunset occurs. This fast is one of the pillars or duties of the faith.

sahlab A hot milky drink.

shabab Means "youth" or "boys." During the intifada, it came to mean youth activists involved in the struggle.

shahada The declaration of faith, or creed, that is a Muslim's statement of the acceptance of God.

suhur The morning meal that occurs before the fast begins during Ramadan.

taqiya A small hat or skullcap.

thaub A long-sleeved, long dress. A traditional dress of Palestinian women.

Acknowledgments

I'm thankful to the following people and institutions who,
through their generous donation of time and resources,
were helpful in research and other ways:

Nivin Qaisi and Nisreen Qaisi for their hospitality and interview.

Muhannad Darwish for his interview and documentary.

James and Linda Herr-Wheeler for their hospitality, photos, interviews, and manuscript reading.

Dave Oberholtzer Lefever, my writer friend, for his encouragement and manuscript reading.

Assaf J. Kfoury and his wife, Irene Gendzier, for their reading of the manuscript.

Mennonite Central Committee

Teaching the Word Ministries

Palestinian Center for the Study of Non-Violence

Dick Doughty and Mohammed El Aydi for the poem.

All those friends and family who listened to me and counseled me throughout the writing of this book, especially in late September 2001.

I also want to acknowledge the following books as helpful sources among the many I used in my research:

Blood Brothers by Elias Chacour. Grand Rapids: Zondervan Press, 1984.

Gaza: Legacy of Occupation: A Photographer's Journey by Dick Doughty and Mohammed El Aydi. Hartford: Kumarian Press, 1995.

A Year in the Intifada: A Personal Account from an Occupied Land by Gloria Emerson. New York: Atlantic Monthly Press, 1991.

An American Feminist in Palestine: The Intifada Years by Sherna Berger Gluck. Philadelphia: Temple University Press, 1994.

Three Mothers, Three Daughters: Palestinian Women's Stories by Michael Gorkin and Rafiqa Othman. Berkeley: University of California Press, 1996.

Drinking the Sea at Gaza: Days and Nights in a Land Under Siege by Amira Hass. New York: Henry Holt, 1996.

Portraits of Palestinian Women by Orayb Aref Najjar and Kitty Warnock. Salt Lake: University of Utah Press, 1992.

Intifada: The Palestinian Uprising — Israel's Third Front by Ze'ev Schiff and Ehud Ya'Ari. New York: Simon and Schuster, 1991.

To the Reader

The history of Gaza is long and complicated. It was ruled by the Philistines and the Israelites during the time of the Bible. Since then it has been part of the Assyrian, Egyptian, Babylonian, Persian, Greek, Ottoman, and British Empires. Between 1948 and 1967, Gaza was controlled by Egypt, and in 1967 it was occupied by Israel. In August 2005, Israeli forces withdrew from Gaza in a stated attempt to give more control to the Palestinian people and their government. However, Israel does not officially recognize the Palestinian government, and Palestine does not officially recognize the Israeli government. This situation has lead to missile attacks into Israel by Hamas, a part of the Palestinian government, and another invasion of Palestine by Israel. There is no peace treaty between Israel and the Palestinians yet, although we can certainly hope that there will be peace some day soon.

Questions for Discussion:

1. At one point in the story Malaak sees an old man with a goat, and it reminds her of a story about her father. What is the story? Why do you think her family history is so important to her?

2. When Malaak comes face-to-face with an Israeli soldier, she seems very frightened. What did she think

would happen? What did you think would happen to her? If you were Malaak, what would you have done? What do you think it would be like to have soldiers from another country stationed in the city where you live?

3. Malaak's brother, Hamid, and his friend Tariq become increasingly involved with a new group of friends. Who are the people they are spending their time with? Why is Malaak frightened of these people? How is Hamid changing? Why do you think he is changing? What do you think Malaak's father would say to Hamid and Tariq if he could speak to them?

4. What is the meaning of the stones on the roof? Why does Malaak bring them down from the roof? What are her brother and Tariq planning to do with the stones? What did you think would happen to the stones? What do you think about what actually happened? Were you surprised?

5. After Hamid is wounded he is taken to a nearby hospital. Where does his mother want him to be taken? Why does she want him to go somewhere else? Where does he end up? What does this tell you about the conditions in Gaza during the time when this novel takes place?

6. While Israeli settlements have been dismantled and Israeli soldiers are no longer stationed inside, the Gaza Strip remains Israeli-occupied territory under

international law, with Israeli troops maintaining control over Gaza's land and sea borders. Movement of people and goods in and out of the Gaza Strip is tightly regulated by the Israeli military. As a result, Gazans often say that they are living under siege. Try to find out something about the living conditions of Gazans today.

7. Some of the people who are living in Gaza now used to live in Israel when it was called Palestine and governed by the British. Some of them are the children and grandchildren of people who used to live in Israel before it became an independent country in 1948. Many of these people live in refugee camps. Some of them want to go back to their old homes and land within Israel. Some want to stay in Gaza. What do you think they should do?

8. There are many Jews living in Israel now who came from other places. Some of them came to live in Israel because they wanted to, while others came because they were no longer welcome in their former countries and had no other place to go. When they first came to Israel they lived in refugee camps, some of them very similar to the ones in Gaza. Today there are no Jews in Israel living in refugee camps. In what way is this similar to the situation in Gaza? In what way is it different?

*For an extended discussion guide,
visit www. candlewick.com*

Cathryn Clinton is the author of several acclaimed
books for children and young adults. She received her master
of fine arts degree from Vermont College.